Friday the Rabbi Wore Lace

Jewish Lesbian Erotica

Edited by
Karen X. Tulchinsky

Friday the Rabbi Wore Lace

Jewish Lesbian Erotica

Edited by
Karen X. Tulchinsky

CLEIS
PRESS

Published in the United States by Cleis Press Inc., P.O. Box 14684, San Francisco, California 94114.
Printed in the United States.
Cover design: Scott Idleman
Text design: Frank Wiedemann
Logo art: Juana Alicia
Front Cover Photo: Melanie Friend
Cover Model: Jamie Gross
First Edition.
10 9 8 7 6 5 4 3 2 1

"La Bruja" was previously published in *Love, Death & Other Disasters*, by Jenifer Levin, Firebrand Books, Ithaca, NY, 1996. "Esther's Story" was previously published in *A Restricted Country*, by Joan Nestle, Firebrand Books, Ithaca, NY, 1987. "The Escape Artist" is an excerpt from the novel *The Escape Artist*, by Judith Katz, Firebrand Books, Ithaca, NY, 1997. "Virgin's Gift" originally appeared in *Best Lesbian Erotica 1997* edited by Tristan Taormino, Cleis Press, 1997. An earlier version of "Love Ruins Everything" was published in *HeatWave* edited by Lucy Jane Bledsoe, Alyson Publications, 1995 and also appears as chapters 1 and 2 in *Love Ruins Everything* a novel, by Karen X. Tulchinsky. "That's Amore" was written by Brooks and Warren, copyright Warner Chappel Music Canada.

Library of Congress Cataloging-in-Publication-Data

Friday the Rabbi wore lace : Jewish lesbian erotica / edited by Karen X. Tulchinsky.
    p.   cm.
   ISBN 1-57344-041-8 (alk.paper)
   1. Lesbian--Sexual behavior--Fiction. 2. American fiction--Jewish authors.
3. Lesbians' writing, American. 4. erotic stories, American. I. Tulchinsky, Karen X.
   PS648.L47 F75 1998
   813' .540803538--ddc21   98-40699
                                                          CIP

Dedication

For Joan Nestle,
a courageous Jewish femme lesbian, who stood on the front lines of
the lesbian sex wars of the '80s, writing and speaking about lesbian
desire, paving the way for the rest of us, and who continues to write
with ferocious honesty.

Acknowledgments

Many thanks to Frédérique Delacoste, Felice Newman, and the staff of Cleis Press for their enthusiasm, hard work, and expertise in bringing this book to publication. Thanks to my friends, family, and colleagues for assistance, support, and encouragement: Tova Fox, Lois Fine, Joan Nestle, Dianne Whelan, Lee McArthur, Maike Engelbrecht, James Johnstone, Lawrence Schimel, Marlys La Brash, Barbara Kuhne, Trigger, Richard Banner, Victoria Chan, and Blaine Kyllo.

Toda Raba to my fiancée, Terrie Akemi Hamazaki, for her love, patience, and unflinching faith in me and to Charlie Tulchinsky-Hamazaki for his own special brand of unconditional love.

Thanks to my parents, Jack and Marion, for sending me to Hebrew school when I was a kid and raising me to be the nice Jewish butch that I am. And of course, many thanks to the wonderful Jewish lesbian writers who contributed their steamy, sensuous, seductive stories.

Contents

Introduction

In 1982 Evelyn Torton Beck published *Nice Jewish Girls: A Lesbian Anthology*, a collection of writings by Jewish dykes. A groundbreaking book: educational for non-Jewish lesbians (and nonlesbian Jews) and most significant, healing for Jewish dykes. Finally, someone was putting those two words, two identities, together in one sentence. Jewish *and* lesbian. Something that had not happened often before then. For Jewish lesbians, this was of monumental importance.

Like most Jewish dykes, I was raised to become a nice Jewish girl who would grow up to marry a nice Jewish boy, preferably a doctor. Imagine my parents' surprise when I came out as a lesbian and they watched helplessly as year after year I became more and more butch, and their hopes and dreams for their second daughter fizzled and died. (Well, I didn't marry one, but I look like a nice Jewish boy. My parents' consolation prize.)

In 1991 my first published story, *Latex and Lube*, was included in *Getting Wet: Tales of Lesbian Seduction*. Surprise, surprise—the narrator of the story was a short, Canadian, Jewish butch. And although there wasn't anything particularly Jewish per se about my story, you could say it was Jewish lesbian erotica. Why? Because I wrote it, and everything I do is informed by my identity as a Jewish dyke. Jewish identity itself, much like queer identity, is a diverse, multilayered, complicated thing that is different for every Jew. It is a religion. And a culture. And a heritage. And a race. And we are interracial. Having moved from one place to another, been kicked out of various countries, and shuffled around all over the world, Jews are perhaps one of the most mixed races on the planet. We are Middle Eastern, European, South American, African, Asian, and North American. And we are mixtures of all of the above. We are religious. We are secular. We are left-wing radical commie hippie pinko queer Jews. And we are conservative right-wing Republican heterosexual married-with-2.5-children-and-a-station-wagon Jewish professionals living in the suburbs. And we are everything in between.

When I put out the call for submissions for an anthology of Jewish lesbian erotica, some people responded with the question, "What is Jewish lesbian erotica?" Try to answer that in fifty words or less. Reminds me of the old joke: ask two Jews a question, get three answers. As I began to receive stories, I saw that as is true of all lesbian erotica, there is not one answer to the question. There are hundreds of answers, thousands. In some of the pieces, the Jewish content is integral to the story, as in Lesléa Newman's "A Religious Experience," about a Yom Kippur spiritual/sexual/psychic connection between two lovers. In other stories, like Jenifer Levin's "La Bruja," a lovely and sad tale of a butch's infatuation with the high femme of her community, or Joan Nestle's "Esther's

Story," set in the late 1950s about a one-night stand between a younger femme and an older butch, the Jewishness of the story is more subtle. Found in the subtext. In the texture. The language. The personality of the central character. In other stories, award-winning author Judith Katz takes us back to a late 1800s Jewish brothel in Buenos Aires, and emerging writer Margarita Miniovitch humorously depicts a woman on the verge of coming out, choosing a hot date with her lesbian co-worker over spending the first night of Chanukah with her lonely mother.

The erotica in the book runs on a continuum of lesbian desire. From the sweet, comical "Knaydle and the Librarian," by Elana Dykewomon, to a Jewish S/M commitment ritual in Karen Taylor's "A Blessing and a Curse," and all points in between.

Jewish lesbian readers will feel at home with the many references to our holidays, food, and culture. Non-Jewish readers will enjoy these hot, steamy, sensuous lesbian stories simply because the writing is great. The authors are from Canada, Israel, England, and the United States, and there is Yiddish, Hebrew, Spanish, and Russian sprinkled throughout.

With humor, heart, and chutzpah, the contributors to the book entertain, arouse, tell tales, and in true Jewish tradition, find joy in the midst of sorrow.

So, recline in a comfortable chair, with a glass of hot tea and a bissel of honey cake, and enjoy the stories. As my bubbe would say (although she's still waiting to dance at my wedding), *Zy gezunt:* you should only live and be well.

Karen X. Tulchinsky
February 1998
Vancouver

A Religious Experience

Lesléa Newman

My girlfriend Melinda, also known as the *shayneh maidel* from Manhattan, has skin the color of a perfectly toasted bagel, lips like lox, and teeth as white as cream cheese. Her eyes are two dark poppy seeds, and her hair is luscious as chocolate *babka*. I could just eat her up, my little *Vildeh Chaya* with her shiksa-straight nose and Gone with the Wind waist, the only woman in the world who makes Vanessa Williams look like chopped liver. But I can't. Not today anyway, because today is Yom Kippur, the one day of the year when my fetching femme won't let me lay a finger on her. And nothing makes a butch hornier than a slap on the wrist followed by those four little words:

"Hands off the merchandise."

For those of you who have strayed from the fold as I have, let me fill you in. Yom Kippur (pronounced "Yum Kip-PAH" by us Noo Yawkers and "Yome Kip-POUR" by the rest of the world) is the most important Jewish holiday of the year. To celebrate it, we Jews refrain from eating, drinking, talking on the phone, riding in a car, working, watching TV, and making love. Some holiday. It's also the day that God (spelled "G-d" by the true chosen people) opens up his little black book and decides who gets to stick around for another year and who gets to kick the bucket. So all of us Yid kids put on our Sunday best (only in our case it's our Saturday best) and schlepp ourselves to shul to atone for our sins. Except for yours truly, of course, who hasn't set foot in a synagogue since 1979, the year I got caught in the coat room nibbling on the neck of the Rabbi's daughter, because I thought it was a sin for such a drop-dead gorgeous girlchik to be sweet sixteen and never been kissed.

So much for religion. I don't really believe in God and all that, but Melinda does. She almost didn't even date me because she thought I was a goy. "Laurie Dellacora," she mulled my name over. "What kind of Jewish name is that?"

"My mother's maiden name is Lipshitz," I told her. "Thank God my parents didn't decide to hyphenate." Then I explained further that my mother's side of the family is Russian Jewish and my father's side is Italian Catholic. Which didn't please Melinda too much, because as she said, she had her heart set on a purebred. But what could she do?—Jewish butches are awfully hard to find. Plus I am quite handsome and charming, if I do say so myself, especially when I want to be. And I definitely wanted to be, the day I met Melinda. Lucky for me the Jews believe that everything is passed down through the motherline and any Rabbi worth his weight in Manishevitz would proclaim me as one of the tribe (as would Hitler, by the way). My parents didn't care all that much about either religion, to tell you the truth, except during the month of December, when we had both a menorah and a Christmas tree in the living room. Which was fine with me, because it meant I got lots of presents. But other than that, I never really cared about religion one way or the other.

Until I met Melinda. Let's just put it this way: if my being a Jew makes her happy, then it makes me happy, too. Melinda likes to celebrate the Sabbath by lighting candles and eating challah, which is A-okay by me. She also likes to get down and dirty on Friday nights (and Saturday mornings, too) because the Jews believe it's a mitzvah to make love on the *Shabbos*. Now there's a tradition I can certainly get behind (and on top of) on a regular basis. We have a lovely little thing going on Friday nights, my Melinda and I. After work we have a nice dinner, and then while I'm doing the dishes, my Sabbath bride whips up an out-of-this-world noodle kugel that she pops into the oven. It takes about an hour to bake, which is just about how long it takes for us to get cooking, too. And somehow, even though we usually have a pretty big supper, an hour later, we're simply starving.

But that's about as far as it goes, when it comes to tradition, no matter how magnificently Zero Mostel sings about it on Melinda's Fiddler on the Roof album. I mean, I'll be the first to admit that Melinda has me wrapped around her little pink-tipped pinky, but the one thing she cannot do, no matter how hard she tries, is convince me to go to shul.

"Are you sure you don't want to come?" she asks this morning, sitting on the edge of our bed, pulling a sheer silk stocking over her shapely thigh.

"I never said I didn't want to come," I reply, sitting down next to her, but as soon as our auras touch, she moves away.

"On Yom Kippur, Laurie? You should be ashamed of yourself," Melinda says, but to tell you the truth, I'm not. In fact, I'm kind of proud of the fact that even after all this time, four years, seven months, and fourteen days, to be exact, my beautiful babe can still drive me delirious with desire. And don't think she doesn't work it. After she's got both her stockings on, Melinda stands to slide her slip over her hips and then bends over to pour her bodacious bosom into her bra. Then she steps into her dress and turns around.

"Will you zip me?" she asks, lifting a yard of hair to show off the back of her neck. Even though we're not really into S/M, I could swear Melinda is getting quite a thrill out of torturing me like this. But if she thinks her little act is going to convince me to go to synagogue and sit stone still on a cold folding chair for hours, listening to some old guy chant in a language I don't understand while my stomach gurgles in harmony (I'm fasting along with Melinda as a sign of solidarity), she's got another thing coming.

"I'm going now," Melinda says, putting on a coat, since the autumn air's a little crisp. "Last call for services."

"I'll pass," I say, coming over to kiss her good-bye, but as soon as I come near her, Melinda backs away.

"Unh-unh-unh," she says, wagging her finger at me. Then she flounces down the steps and, knowing I'm watching her, moons me when she reaches the bottom. And since Melinda has nothing on underneath her holiday frock except a garter belt, I have to hang onto the banister to keep from falling down the stairs. She laughs, straightens up, and leaves, locking the door behind her.

So, now what? There's nothing to do but go back to bed, since Melinda didn't have to work too hard to convince me to take the day off. "Yom Kippur is supposed to be a complete Sabbath," she said. So, fine. Just because I don't observe the religion doesn't mean I shouldn't enjoy the perks. I doze off for a while, then sit up and watch a little TV. But it's no use. All I can think about is my Melinda. Those dark, dark eyes. Those pouty pink lips. Those big beautiful breasts. And that absolutely amazing ass.

Well, why not? Here I am in bed, and I can't think of one good reason not to let my fingers do the walking. I mean, what the hell, I've got all day. And here's something I don't understand: if, as Melinda says, Yom Kippur is a complete *Shabbos*, the holiest day of the year, the Grand Poobah of Sabbaths, and ordinarily it's a mitzvah to make love on the Sabbath, then why wouldn't it be a blessing to spend all day in bed with your beloved? Like, let's be consistent here, you know what I mean?

I take off my T-shirt and boxer shorts and start by just running my hands lightly up and down my body. I'm strong and in pretty good shape, if I do say so myself. I'm not doing too badly in the flab department either, except for some recent developments around my stomach area, but still, I'll be damned before I start drinking Miller Lite. I don't want to be stick-skinny or anything—I don't find thin women attractive in the least, and I'm glad my Melinda is nice and *zaftig*—I just want to stay in shape. Mostly so I can sling my sweetie over my shoulder and bundle her off to bed the way she likes. And the way I'd like to, right now.

But like it or not, this is a solo performance. I rub my palms around my nipples in small circles and wait for them to get hard.

It takes a while because, frankly, I don't have the kind of body I'm attracted to. I'm pretty flat, unlike Melinda, who's a size 38D, which I always tell her stands for Delicious. Melinda can come just from having me lick and suck her breasts, which amazes me. I, of course, can come just from making her come, which amazes Melinda, but hey, what can I say? It's a butch thing.

I'm not exactly getting turned on here, so I shut my eyes and pretend my hands are touching the body of my beloved. Which means I have to leave the breast department and travel south. I move my hands down my body and start stroking the insides of my thighs, which, like Melinda's, are smooth and silky as puppy ears. Then I start petting my pubic hair and pulling on it gently, the way that drives Melinda wild. I mean, when I do it to her, of course; I would never touch myself in front of my girlfriend, though I like it when she touches herself in front of me. The first time I asked her if she'd ever do that, she just smiled and took her top off. In fact, she kind of got off on it. It's a femme thing, I guess. At least, that's what Melinda tells me.

I actually start to get a little worked up, so I use my left hand to make small circles around my clit. Ah, instant relief, like an itch that's just dying to be scratched. And then my right hand gets a little bored, I guess, because there's no other way to explain what happens next. All of a sudden, my middle finger sneaks in where no one has gone before. My snatch, the final frontier.

Wow, I'm surprised at how hot and wet and soft I am inside. Well, what were you expecting, sandpaper? I ask myself. I've never really penetrated myself before, or let Melinda, even though she tries sometimes and pouts when I say she can't. But I don't know, it seems too much a femme thing to let someone in like that. I almost can't stand doing it to myself, if you want to know the truth, so I make sure my eyes are shut tight, so I can keep pretending I'm touching my lady.

I keep the finger that's inside still the way Melinda likes, and I keep rubbing my clit back and forth with my other hand. I'm breathing pretty heavily now, and before I can even think about it, I slide another finger inside. Woah, I guess there's room at the inn, because before I even know what I'm doing, finger number three joins the rest of the crowd. Dare I go for four? No, I have a better idea. When my girl's really hot and open for me, she likes my thumb inside, all the way up to the fleshy part that joins it to my hand, and my middle finger up her butt. I go for it, and before I can even say, "Come for me, baby," my hips are moving, my legs are shaking, and I'm practically drooling all over myself—but I don't care. Thank God there's no one around to see me like this. No, wait a minute. I wish there were someone around to witness me losing total control. But not just any someone. A certain someone named Melinda. I know how much I love her when I see her giving me everything she's got. I wonder if she would feel the same way. Or would she laugh at me and demand I turn in my butch card?

"Melinda, Melinda!" I yell as I come and come and come. It takes a few minutes for me to stop shaking and a few more after that to catch my breath. When I'm finally my usual calm, cool, collected self, I remove my fingers and thumb from my various orifices and reach for Melinda, but of course she's not here. That's the thing about masturbation: afterward there's no one to hold and squeeze and say "I love you" to while you look deep into her eyes. There's no one to stroke and pet and whisper sweet nothings to while she rests her head on your shoulder. There's no one to even say "Wow, I never knew you could come like that" to, so I get out of bed and say it to myself in the bathroom mirror. "Wow. I never knew you could come like that."

"There's a lot of things about me that you don't know," I say to my reflection as I wash my hands. I mean, I've always been the one who got off on pleasing my lover, and I've never gotten any complaints. But I know Melinda wishes she could do some of the things to me that I just did to myself. I swore long ago that I'd never flip. But now that I've flipped myself, who knows? After all, it is a new year. Maybe change is in the air.

So, is Melinda going to stay in shul all day or what? It's only a little after 1:00, which means I have five hours to go until the holiday is over. Officially Yom Kippur ends at sunset, but since we stopped eating at 6:30 yesterday, I convinced Melinda we could break the fast at 6:30 today. I wonder if that means we can fuck at 6:30, too. I certainly hope so. You'd think I'd have had enough for one day, but for some reason I'm hornier than ever. In fact, I can hardly wait to get my hands on that girl.

I take a shower, get dressed, make the bed, listen to some music, and wait for Melinda to get home. When she finally walks in at 5:15, I go to scoop her up in my arms, but she is too excited to sit still.

"Laurie, you won't even believe what happened to me in temple today," she says, fluttering all over the room. Maybe the poor girl is delirious from lack of food. I know I am, not to mention lack of caffeine. "So, I'm sitting there, right, just minding

my own business, reading along with the prayer book and everything, and then like halfway through the service, the rabbi
stands and the ark is open, so the whole congregation stands,
too. And then this new cantor goes up to the bima, and she
starts to sing and she has the most amazing voice, I swear, it's
like an angel's in the room. I was really wishing you were there
to hear her, Laurie, and then it was almost like you were there,
right next to me. I could, like, feel your presence or something.
And I was swaying to the cantor's voice, and then my whole
body just started to shake and shudder and I had to sit down
even though the ark was still open, because I thought I was
going to faint. My heart was beating really fast, I could barely
catch my breath, and my face was all red, almost like when,
almost like, well, you know." Melinda looks down demurely.

"Wait a minute, was this cantor femme or butch?" I fold my
arms in a huff. Maybe I should have gone to synagogue with
Melinda after all.

"She was a femme, silly. Anyway, that's not the point. The
point is, these, like, waves started rippling through my body and
all I could think about was you, like I could practically hear your
voice, like you were calling me or something, and then I sat back
down and I swear, my whole chest was all flushed, like it is after
we make love. It was totally amazing, like some sort of religious
experience or something."

Am I good, or what? I think, my heart starting to beat fast,
too. "So, um, like what time was this?" I ask, trying to sound
nonchalant.

"What time?" Melinda looks up at the clock. "I don't know.
Why?"

"Just curious."

"I don't know, let me think." Melinda tilts her head. "It must have been around one o'clock, because then the rabbi started his sermon, and he always does his sermons around one."

"I see," I say, more to myself than to her.

"So, what did you do today?" Melinda asks, coming to sit down next to me on the couch, but not too close, since the sun has yet to set.

"Oh, not much. Just hung around. Thought about you," I say, putting my arm across her shoulder.

"Laurie." Melinda rolls her eyes, but she isn't really annoyed, because she doesn't pull away. "God, I'm starving, aren't you?"

"You betcha. What are you in the mood for?"

"Well, I bought a bagel-and-lox spread to break the fast with, but what I really feel like eating is a huge piece of noodle kugel. What about you?"

"I'd kill for a kugel right now," I say.

"I know," Melinda jumps up. "I'll put one in the oven, and by the time it's ready, we'll be able to eat." She bustles around the kitchen, putting up water to boil for the noodles, beating eggs, melting butter, and before I can even offer to help the *Shvitzing* Gourmet, our dinner's sizzling in the oven.

"Will you help me do the dishes?" Melinda asks, wiping her hands on a dish towel.

"I have a better idea," I say, coming up behind her and putting my arms around her waist. "Let's get into bed while it's baking."

"Laurie," Melinda says again, but I can tell she's weakening. Her eyes are all big like they are when she wants me.

"C'mon, love," I whisper in her ear, letting my tongue linger. "I've got a surprise for you."

"Ooh, what is it?" Melinda squeals. Melinda loves surprises.

"You'll see," I say taking her by the hand.

"Is it something to eat?" she asks, her stomach rumbling.

"Not really," I answer, "but it's finger-licking good."

And it is.

The First Night

Margarita Miniovich

The Friday Paula Creen leaned on my desk with her elbows and wished me Merry Christmas, I knew I was in love.

"Thanks, Merry Christmas to you too," I said, fully aware that tonight was the first night of Chanukah and thinking that instead of staring at the smooth black buttons of her double-breasted suit, trying to imagine the texture of her skin underneath the cream silk of her shirt, I should have been enlightening her about our cultural differences. I should have been telling her that I'm Jewish in a firm but friendly tone, explaining that although some Jews have been known to have such things as "Chanukah bushes" in their homes, I was certainly not one of them—my mother would have killed me. I should have told her that I resented her assumption that I would be happy to receive even the bestest of wishes for the celebration of the birth of Jesus Christ, unless I was one of those "Jews for Jesus" freaks, which, incidentally, I would have considered becoming in that instant, if that's what she'd wanted.

My conversion thoughts were interrupted by three phone lines ringing at once. Three red lights lit up the white telephone, like Christmas. I had to answer; that's what I got paid for.

"It's my favorite time of year," I said instead, "I love all those presents and chocolates."

I don't know why I said that: chocolate gives me zits and getting presents makes me shy and uncomfortable—I've always hated that tense silence that falls in the room when you open a present, trying not to ruin the happy-face wrapping paper, the presenter watching you intently, catching your every wince and twitch, waiting for *Oh, I love it, thank you!* even if it is a yellow polyester potholder.

"I can't stand Christmas," Paula said, straightening up. "My dad drinks and armwrestles with my brother until they break a dish or two, and my mother picks up broken glass all night. I'd rather be at work any day. They drive me crazy."

She stretched her arms out and behind her back, bending her neck to one side and then the other.

"I know exactly what you mean," I said, watching her neck. Her blouse was unbuttoned enough for me to see a thin blue vein that ran from her collarbone to the underside of her chin. I had an insane impulse to kiss it, to feel its pulsing softness. I chewed on the eraser end of the pencil. Two of the red lights gave up and went out, but the third was persistent.

"Sorry, I have to get that," I said, reaching for the phone, hoping she'd wait.

"That's okay. I have to go anyway," Paula said, "Do you still want to go dancing tonight, Fraulein Dianne?" and looked into my eyes in a way that made my crotch twitch. I hoped it wasn't because of the German—I was having enough of an identity crisis as it was. "Hey, it rhymes," she added.

"Yes, I want to, very much," I said into the receiver, "I mean, good afternoon, can I help you?"

"Good, I'll see you tonight at ten, in front of the bar," she said as she left the room.

I pressed my thighs together really hard. *Oh God, please make me look like Demi Moore, just for tonight*, I prayed, writing down that Mr. Klein had called for Mr. Devries.

My notepad was covered with pencil sketches of a woman's profile, all resembling Paula's.

Earlier that fall I'd dropped out of a social work program at Ryerson College. I had a hard time packaging people's problems into neat, identifiable parcels that snugly fit textbook definitions and could, therefore, be solved if you followed certain rules. I knew life was messier than that. I knew that the chill in my chest from my sister dying in a car accident ten years ago was permanent and could not be helped by "caring professionals." I considered applying to an art college, preferably somewhere far away, like Arizona. I had a thing about Arizona—I imagined adventures of the Barbara Kingsolver kind, which would warm me up like good scotch, the sun with its moist, penetrating heat, sunsets the color of tangerines and plums, and cactuses shaped like contortionists. I didn't know if my occasional sketching and persistent daydreaming about becoming an artist was sufficient to get me accepted to art school. So, in the meantime I did nothing except listen to my mother's grumbling about how irresponsible I'd been to leave college and about how when she was my age she'd already had me and was going to night school, divorcing my father, and working, all at the same time. I usually held the phone away from my ear until I heard silence on her end and then would ask her if I could borrow some money until my next paycheck. That was her cue to groan and tell me that no, she would not lend me money, that would be enabling me to continue my life of chaos, but I could come over for Shabbat dinner. I would remind her that it was only Tuesday, and I was already hungry, and she would say in her very firm tone, "Dianne Horovitz, stop this foolishness, no daughter of mine has ever gone hungry. There are plenty of canned foods you could buy for under a dollar. You have to learn to budget and save. We're having barbecued chicken on Friday, and don't be late. I want to light the candles on time." Sometimes, after these conversations, feeling guilty and furious, I would picture myself in Arizona, as a cactus—thick and prickly and mute, unbending under the scorching sun.

In October I got myself this receptionist job, where I practiced the above-mentioned qualities: the *thick* part came easy since I'd gained ten pounds on Kraft dinners in the past year, and *prickly* had been my middle name since kindergarten, where I made Mrs. Brianny cry when I bit her thumb with all my might for brushing out the tangles in my curly hair, pulling really hard and telling me that in her time girls with *that kind of hair* had it ironed every morning. The *mute* part was coming along nicely. I figured that way I could keep this job for a few months and save enough money for a plane ticket to Arizona. I'd been working in this interior design company's reception room for three months now and was running out of things to do to keep myself awake for eight hours a day. The room was full of green velveteen armchairs for the clients, tasteful Japanese prints on peach-colored walls, and fast-moving designers who ran around with pencils stuck behind their ears like bikers with Marlboros. Crossword puzzles, feminist theory books, Ruth Rendell's mysteries, and talking to my friend Jenny for hours about her therapy were starting to bore me. I envied Paula, in her gray tailored suits and men's shoes, for knowing what she wanted to do with her life and doing it—she was one of the best interior designers in the company, and they paid her a lot of money. I knew because I stuffed the envelopes with everyone's paychecks. She arrived early, left late, ate lunch in her office, and never told me to say she was in a meeting when she wasn't. She kept her pencils dangling from a buttonhole of her jacket. She was everything I wanted to be but couldn't quite manage: happy, tall, slim, straight-haired, and dark-eyed. She was one of those girls I'd hated in high school. I figured she probably got A's in gym. I'd always had big thighs, frizzy hair, blue eyes the shade of boring; I used to change in the bathroom for gym classes; and I got laughed at by the other girls in ninth grade when I couldn't jump over the damn horse, my stomach twisting every time I got near it.

Paula also had a cute half-smile, one corner of her mouth turned slightly up, sly and boyish, that made me want, for the first time in my twenty-four years, to kiss a girl.

I began fantasizing about that mouth in November, my hand slowing down to a freeze in the middle of recording a message on the pink office pad, picturing the dark red curl of her lips, imagining pressing against them, my tongue smoothing out her smirk, her tongue pushing inside my mouth, the warmth, the first gasp. I had no idea what was supposed to follow, but that imagined kiss was enough to make my panties wet and make me forget who'd called and what message I was supposed to pass on to whom. I didn't know what the hell was going on. I'd taken enough women's studies courses to know there were women who slept with other women. Lesbians were even envied, usually, by the straight girls in class, who'd say loudly and with an almost believable pinch of regret, "Oh, I really wish I were a lesbian, all men are scum!" I never wished that, could never really understand the attraction. Although I'd never felt *in love*, I had *deconstructed* love enough times in college to feel relief at the absence of its pull in my life. I liked guys, thought of sex as sport, good for my inner thigh muscles, and was sleeping with Andy and Jacob at the moment, once a week each. My mother liked Jacob and took every opportunity to remind me that if I wanted to wear her wedding dress I had to lose some weight.

One November morning I got to work at 8:30 am. I was grumpy, more so than usual because I had been deprived of half an hour of the thing I appreciated most in life—sleep. The day before, Mr. Devries, one of my numerous bosses, had asked me to type up a report he needed for a 9:00 meeting. While I was busy trying to figure out his handwriting—his *t*'s looked like *i*'s and his *n*'s were the same as *m*'s—the front door opened and Paula rushed in.

"Oh god, I'm late," she said, taking off her charcoal cashmere coat. It was covered with a white film of new snow. "Is he here already?" The way the snow had fallen on her hair made it look like she had on one of those lacy head coverings that women wore to shul. Her cheeks were red from the cold, and she was looking right into my eyes.

"Who?" I asked.

"Devries! We have a meeting this morning and I'm supposed to pitch to a very *importanto* client."

Paula had a habit of inserting foreign words into her speech, which usually made me smile.

"No," I said, "I'm the only one here."

She moved really close to my desk.

"How do I look?" she asked. Her short dark hair was shiny with that just-polished cherrywood gloss, her skin almost translucent, her lips moist from the melting snow.

"*Fantastico*," I said, feeling a strange warmth expanding in my belly. She bent over my desk. I could smell her perfume. It smelled like new grass.

"Good. I believe you." She gave me a long look. "*Ciao*," she said, and went upstairs.

I had to catch my breath. This had never happened to me before. Not with guys, not with anyone. I'd never felt my blood rush to my face like that and then down between my legs and back up again. I couldn't get her face out of my mind all day. I ran out of the office at 5:00 on the dot, terrified that I'd see her and that she'd see me: the wanting in my eyes. *I'm not a lesbian, I can't be*, I kept thinking on the bus ride home. It's not that I wanted to sleep with women, it was just something about her that made my face hot. At home I made myself come four times in a row, imagining a small studio in the Arizona desert, Paula posing for me on a riser, naked, her nipples erect, one of her hands on her cunt, touching herself. I saw myself trying to concentrate on the sketch and drawing her wet, dark pubic hair over and over. I saw Paula's face as she put a finger inside herself, twisting her hips, closing her eyes as she came. Afterward, I was so horny I called Andy to come over and fuck me. He wasn't surprised. I'd called him with that request before, and he always rushed over, ready and able. That night I kept squeezing his chest and sucking his nipples, making them hard and raw, until he asked me to stop. I told him to leave after because I had to get up early.

The next morning it was snowing hard. I waited twenty minutes for the rush-hour bus. Still, I was at work at 8:30. I wanted to see Paula come in and shake the snow off her hair. I had worn my favorite gray mohair sweater, the one that made my eyes look deep and sad. I didn't care that I'd sweat like crazy all day. She was surprised to see me and said, "That's a nice sweater, really brings out your eyes."

I said, "Thanks. I can give it to you after I move to Arizona. I won't be needing it there." I had no idea why I said that.

"Now, that's a place I'd like to see," she answered. "Maybe I'll come and visit you there. What do you think?"

"I think…," I didn't know what I thought—she had taken me by surprise. "I think I'd like…you'd like it there."

She paused for a second, looking at me, and I was terrified she could see my fantasy from the night before in my eyes.

"You just never know, do you…" she said, finally.

I had no idea what she meant, but I spent that whole day daydreaming about her silk blouse, the color of sand, and my hands searching for hot pearls in the dark green water. I turned to a fresh page in my notepad and drew hands dipped in what looked like furry moss, over and over.

Getting to work early became a habit. I wasn't even missing my sleep that much. And the compliments I got from Mr. Devries about my exemplary attitude raised my hopes for a Christmas bonus. I went shopping, spending that money in advance, and bought some new clothes. I developed a craving for soft, silky textures against my skin and colors I'd never worn before, like deep reds and violets. I had even begun to use conditioner in my hair, the same kind my mother used, which turned her frizz, identical to mine, into miraculous curls that everyone raved about. My friend Jenny commented that I must be either turning into a yuppie or sleeping with a rich guy. I also noticed that Paula would sometimes pass by my desk and slow down, almost imperceptibly, as if wanting to say something.

"I'm going to P-town in March," she whispered in my ear one morning, about three weeks into my new and improved work ethic. I just nodded, feeling her breath on my neck. I didn't want to say anything for fear of letting out a moan.

"Do you know what that is?" she asked, straightening up.

"No, not really," I said, feeling really foolish.

She smiled and ran her fingers through her hair.

"Come here," she gestured to me with her free hand. I leaned across my desk and stretched out my neck, like a duck.

"It's a resort town," she said, "A gay resort. I'm a lesbian." She stopped fussing with her hair and became very still, like a statue. I pulled my neck back into my shoulders.

"Oh," I said, "I knew that." It popped out of my mouth just like that. I had no idea where it came from.

"You did, did you?" Paula said, "I thought you knew. But still, you just never know…"

That night after work I went to the women's bookstore and asked the thin-lipped woman behind the counter to point me in the direction of their lesbian section. I tried to sound as casual as I could. I found what I was looking for, paid in cash, and stuffed the receipt deep into my coat pocket. I wanted to start reading on the subway, but I was afraid somebody would see. By the time I got home, I was so horny and wet that I lay down on my couch and without even thinking of food, which was totally out of character for me, unzipped my pants. I put my hand inside over my crotch and felt the wetness through my panties. With one hand rubbing my clit, at first very lightly, teasing myself, making me swell and rise up for more, the book in the other, then harder and faster, the lips of my cunt parting, I read about women licking each other's pussies in backseats of cars, fucking each other with fingers, fists, and tongues in dark alleyways, behind husbands' backs, and underneath the tablecloths of chic restaurants. I put two fingers inside myself and rocked back and forth, with my thumb rubbing the tip of my clit until I came so hard that the words *she fucked her hard until she came* blurred and I let the book fall onto my belly.

You want to sleep with a woman, a little voice in my head said with a kind of certainty I'd never heard before. As I was falling asleep my stomach cramped, and I dreamt that the sleeves of my mother's wedding dress kept getting caught between my thighs.

"Do you want to go dancing with me sometime?" Paula asked on a Tuesday in late December. My eyes were sore from staring at the computer screen for the past two hours.

"Yeah, but I've never been to a place like that before," I said. And then, instantly regretted it.

"A place like what? Are you afraid of getting eaten up, little girl?" Paula's voice was very quiet. "Little Red Riding Hood, are you wondering why I have such big teeth?"

If she only knew.

"Stop it," I said, surprised that I had the guts to talk back to her, "That's not what I meant." My hands were shaking, but I was looking right at her.

"Okay, *muchacha*," she said, smiling wickedly, "I forgive you this time."

I almost said *thank you*.

"How about this Friday night?"

"Friday is fine," I said, trying to figure out what I would tell my mother, since this Friday was the first night of Chanukah and we've always had dinner and lit the first candle together. No Mom, it's not your cooking, I just need to go and be fucked by a woman I hardly know anything about, but you understand, don't you, Mom?

I called my mother and told her I was coming down with a very contagious flu that was going around the office and should stay in bed.

"You don't eat enough vegetables," my mother said, "You're way too susceptible to other people's germs."

I took a cab to the Scratch.

"911 Jarvis Street, please" I said to the cab driver, afraid to say the bar's name aloud, in case he knew it was a lesbian bar.

I got out of the cab, and I thought my heart would stop and never start again when I saw her. In tight black jeans, a black turtleneck sweater, and army boots, she looked untouchable and mesmerizing. I realized I'd only seen her in office gear before. I didn't know if I should shake her hand or give her a hug or just nod my head hello in a dignified manner.

"So, are you ready?" she asked, eyeing me.

"Of course I am," I said, deciding on the nod, "I'm not the sort of girl who changes her mind at the last moment." Oh god, what the hell am I saying?

"That's my kind of *mamelah*," Paula said and smiled. It was the first time I'd heard her use a Yiddish word. Not bad, I thought, and decided not to think about my mother eating cold *latkes* alone in her apartment.

Paula held the door for me as we walked in. The music was so loud the floor vibrated under our feet. As I checked my coat, I sensed Paula's eyes on my back.

"Not bad for your first time," she said into my ear. I looked into the mirror on the wall and saw the black leather miniskirt, my newest acquisition, the cream low-cut top, and my curly hair falling over my eyes. My legs looked good in black pantyhose. At least in the dark. I didn't know what to do with my hands. I should have brought a purse; then I would have had something to hold on to.

"Just a minute," she said, "I have to talk to someone. She works in the coat check. A friend of mine. Don't you move an inch."

She went behind the waist-high partition and whispered something into the ear of a very tall, big woman in a blue sweatshirt. The woman laughed, nodded, and looked in my direction.

I turned away and saw women dancing, moving their bodies, in public, in ways I'd felt free enough to do only in the privacy of my own bed. Paula came out and took my hand. Like it was the most natural thing in the world. I forgot to breathe.

"Come on," she said.

On the dance floor she let go of my hand. You're on your own, girl, I thought. The song had no words, but the beat was steady. There were women all around us. A couple nearby held hands and danced slowly, holding each other and kissing, even to the fast beat of the song. I tried not to stare, but couldn't resist. I moved to the music, feeling my thighs, in silky pantyhose, rub against each other. Paula danced with her hips, swaying side to side, taking small steps with her feet. She had the kind of hidden energy when she moved that made you want to come close and breathe it in. Once in a while she'd look at me and smile. After the third song, she whispered, "Come," and took my hand again. Her hand was hot. She led me back to the coat-check room.

"Follow me," she said. As if I could have done anything but.

Paula opened the partition, and we walked into the room filled with coats and jackets. The big woman grinned as we squeezed by her.

Behind a green, down-filled jacket, by the back wall, Paula took me by the shoulders, leaned me against the wall, and turned my face toward hers. She kissed me. Her lips were soft and cool, her arms were around my back, and I could feel her breasts under her sweater, pressing against mine. Her tongue outlined my mouth and then it was inside, finding mine, our mouths pressed together, her lips hard and demanding, mine opening, wanting her. I felt her hands on my ass, circling and squeezing the leather. I pushed my ass out toward her hands and danced to the beat of the blaring music, moving my hips in small circles, while her fingers slid underneath my skirt.

"I'm going to fuck you, you know that?" she said into my ear. "And there's not a thing you can do about it."

I nodded my head. This is how one loses one's mind, I thought, aware of the sleeves, buttons, belts, and music surrounding us. I was sweating. Paula's hands were inside my nylons, and I writhed to get my cunt closer to her fingers. My hands found her breasts and I moaned. They felt exactly how I'd imagined them, and I wanted them in my mouth.

"So impatient, aren't you?" she said, and kissed my neck slowly, every lick a sweet sting, making my thighs slippery. She took my wrists and pulled them off her breasts, holding them tight by my sides. She slid my nylons down, and her hand was finally where I'd craved it most.

"Aren't you oh-so-wet," she said. "Straight girls like it standing up straight, I hear."

I didn't care, I just wanted her inside me. My cunt pulsed and pushed itself up against her hand. She parted my lips and put her finger on my clit. I thought I'd die. I wanted to come, but she didn't move, just held it there, while her other hand found my breasts. Her lips were on my nipples, sucking, licking. I moved my clit against her finger, faster and faster until I was about to come. She took her hand away and I thought I'd start crying. I let out a sound.

"Shh," she put her wet finger against my lips, "You have to be very quiet, or you'll get nothing."

I took her finger into my mouth and sucked like my life depended on it. I was pinned to the wall by her tongue moving over my nipples. With her other hand she hiked up my skirt and parted my legs. Her fingers entered me slowly. I squeezed my cunt, afraid she'd stop again, but she didn't. Her mouth on my breasts, her finger like a life-force in my mouth, she pushed deep inside me, pulled out, then in again, over and over, fucking me, until I forgot where I was, attached only to her fingers pulsing inside like a second hand on a clock, making me alive one second at a time, in, out, until my cum was running down my thighs and her arm.

We could hear the tall woman, just a few coats away, telling someone it cost a dollar for the coat check.

Paula walked me to the cab, her arm around my shoulders. My legs were shaking.

"I guess that was your Christmas present," she said, opening the cab door for me.

"Actually, that was my Chanukah present," I answered, getting in the backseat.

"Oh, shit, how come you didn't tell me that before?" She looked upset.

"I'm telling you now."

"That's even better," she said, "That means that was only your first present, then. You have six more to go."

"Seven," I said, "Not counting tonight."

"Let's make it nine, okay?" She blew me a kiss as she shut the cab door.

At home, before falling asleep, I lit the first Chanukah candle, making a wish. I cupped my hands around the flame and felt its steady heat filling my hands, flowing up my arms, into my chest, and once there, curling up like a cat and deciding to stay.

The Missing Letter

Gabrielle Glancy

Facts

"My business is circumference," Emily Dickinson wrote. First of all, she is one of America's great poets and any halfway decent work of literature should include her. It happens too that she's on my mind. Just this week I found myself telling my classes about her. I told them how she published four poems in her lifetime but wrote over nine hundred. I told them how the poems were written in a precise slant, every letter perfectly aligned with the one before it with a rigor not just quintessentially New England, but downright deliberate. That woman knew what she was doing.

Imagine Dickinson rolling up that bundle of poems, tying a ribbon around it, and putting it in a chest in her attic. That's what she did, apparently. Did she have a sense of her tremendous worth as a poet? Was she putting them away for posterity?

But the other, more practical reason I bring her up is because

I want to revise Dickinson's words to my own end-of-the-millennium standards: my business is facts.

The Facts in Chronological Order

1. I met Vera through a personal ad.
2. We spent six weeks together. Many things happened, among which, I fell in love with her.
3. I went to New York, then Russia, then New York.
4. I did the man on the plane the night before I came back to San Francisco.
5.   I came back to San Francisco.
6. Vera came over to my house that very evening.
7. The dog yelped wildly and ran around in a lopsided circle chasing his ear.
8. We took him to Emergency Pet Hospital. A foxtail had somehow weaseled its way into his tympanic membrane. It needed to be surgically removed. We could pick him up in a few hours, the doctor said.
9. We came home and made love. The vet called to say the dog was ready.
10. We picked him up from Emergency Pet Hospital.
11. We came home and slept.
12. Vera left before dawn to pick up her mother so they could stand in line to register as refugees.
13. I called Vera. I said, "It was sweet with you last night. What are you doing tonight?"
14. She said, "I'm busy."

15. I said, "What are you doing tomorrow night?"
16. She said, "I'm busy then too,"
17. "Okay," I said. "What are you doing Sunday night?"
18. She said, "Let's speak on Sunday night and figure it out then."
19. I said, "Are you seeing someone else?"
20. She said, "I wrote you a letter."
21. I said, "You're not seeing someone else, are you?"
22. "I wrote you a letter." She said, "Do you really want to know?"
23. I said, "Do I really want to know?"
24. She said, "Yes."
25. I said, "Yes, I really want to know. YOU'RE NOT SEE-ING SOMEONE ELSE, ARE YOU?"
26. She said, "I wrote you a letter."
27. I said, "You wrote me a letter?"
28. She said, "Yes."
29. I said, "OhmyGod, I can't believe this is happening."
30. I said, "The painter?"
31. She said, "No."
32. I said, "The sweet, kind woman?"
33. She said, "No."
34. I said, "Jeannie Friedman?"
35. She said, "Yes."
36. I said, "OhmyGod!"
37. I said, "How long has this been going on?"
38. She said nothing.
39. I said, "All this time?"
40. She said nothing.

41. I said, "How many times have you slept with her?"
42. She said, "That's private."
43. I was on the verge of tears, but I composed myself and gave her a chance to come back to me by saying something that resembled the following: I love you. I'm sorry if I've done something to hurt you.
44. More conversation followed, which I can't bear to recount.
45. At some point, she said, "You can say whatever to me bad you want."
46. I said, "I have nothing bad to say to you."
47. Silence.
48. I said, "I have nothing more to say to you. I'm going to hang up the phone."
49. I hung up the phone and cried into my hands.
50. Vera was gone.

It must be noted at this point that Vera was nineteen years old and I was forty-one. According to all accounts, that is, to everything she told me, she was a virgin when I met her and I was her first.

After the Facts

Since July 22, she is nowhere to be found. I've spent two weeks, day and night, looking for her. I have combed the streets of San Francisco. I went to Herman's Stationers, the place from which Vera sent her faxes. The woman there, a very lanky bleached blond in her twenties, said yes, she remembered a young Russian woman, tall, slender, wavy auburn hair, who had come to send or pick up faxes every day for two weeks between the dates of July 8 and July 22, but that no, she had not seen her. I went to 2020 39th Avenue. I knocked. I rang the bell, I spoke to the tenants upstairs. The place was clean—musty, but clean. And it was empty. No Lena. No Kostya. No Vera. In fact, there was not a trace of them ever having lived there.

I had a sense I was in a dream.

Detail: Item 9: We came home and made love. The vet called to say the dog was ready.

I want to retrace the steps of the last night more closely—perhaps there is something hidden in the facts we have not yet seen. Not only did the dog have a foxtail lodged in his tympanic membrane, but my car, we noticed as we tried to drive it, had a flat.

Luckily, Vera had driven over to my house that night in her 1982 Chevy Cavalier. Spray-painted white, the car listed to one side like some huge limping horse or a boat fighting not to capsize in a vicious wind.

I drove.

Vera sat with Huck, whom I tried to explain to her was a cavalier King Charles spaniel, on her lap.

"Get it?" I said, "cavalier?"

She didn't get the joke. Nor was she thrilled to be holding the dog. He was injured and reactive and she was afraid, I found out then, of animals. Her natural sympathy or lack thereof was apparent. For my part, truth be told, I felt proud to have her holding him. We seemed like a somewhat odd, happy family, then, on the way to do what needed to be done.

We were the only ones at the pet hospital—after all, it was past midnight—so Huck was immediately admitted. We were asked to wait outside the door. Soon after, a squat man with a mustache came in with a ferret and a shoe box. The ferret had, as it were, ferreted into the sleeve of his coat, but he carried the shoe box, lined with flowery tissues, just in case. "His house," he said to us. While he was checking in, Vera and I looked at each other as if to say, "Strange guy." He was a strange guy. The cold fluorescent light blanched his face even more and made the little bit of hair he had on his head seem almost sinister. He looked as if he had walked out of a Peter Sellers movie, a less debonair version of Inspector Clouseau.

Vera stood by the counter, smoking a cigarette, and I stood in front of her, almost, but not quite against her, feeling the warmth of her hips against my ass. She leaned over at one point and put her cheek to my ear, blowing smoke out over the left side of my head.

In a matter of minutes, Dr. Gerber, a bleached blond wearing a white labcoat, came out to say we needed to leave the dog—surgery was necessary to remove the foxtail—but that we could call later to see when he was ready. Without hesitation, Vera and I agreed we'd go home and wait, walked past the counter where the man was signing in his ferret, and got back in the car.

We drove in silence. Vera was an expert at silence, and I had come to expect it. I knew, as one knows these things, that we would go home and make love. At some point, after breathing and sighing, breathing and sighing, I put my hand on her leg.

The air between us was heavy with a tension I assumed was lust. And so, the silence was a kind of foreplay, in my mind, at least, torturous and exquisite, that served to fuel our desire.

Once we were home, Vera stood behind me in the kitchen, her tall body pressing me forward, moving me in the direction of the wall. Again she breathed into my ear, bending around me, pressing me harder now, until I was against the wall, my own breath steaming up the wood.

"Let's go to bed," I said. She was reaching around and unbuttoning my jeans. "Don't you want to lie down?"

Before I could utter another word, her mouth was upon my mouth.

She had opened the door ahead of me and pushed me down on the bed, all the while kissing me, working my body with her wild and active hands, pulling at my hair.

What followed was perhaps the hottest sex we ever had. In a matter of minutes, she had taken off my jeans. In her left hand she held my hair and pinned me to the bed. Half her weight was on me. Her right hand made its way to my wetness, teased and taunted, then skillfully slid inside. She was marvelously deft and aggressive. Her lovely, strong, square jaw and brown eyes shone in the street light that shafted through the window. I could not tell at moments whether she was male or female, whether I was liquid or solid, floating or lying down, caught in the whirlwind that was between us.

Needless to say, she brought me expertly to orgasm. Where her hand failed, her mouth triumphed. She flicked and sucked at me, ceased to move, then picked up wildly. I came into a pillow I grabbed to muffle my cries.

"I am so in love with you!" I said after, panting. "So, so, so in love with you!" And then, because I knew she would feel it more deeply if I said it in Russian, I shivered out, "*Ya tak tibya lioblioo!*"

Vera sighed a heavy sigh and looked—I would have to say, questioningly—into my eyes. I was about to ask her what the matter was when the phone rang. Dizzy, drunk with pleasure and exhaustion, I fumbled for the receiver.

"The dog's ready," I heard a voice say.

"Thanks," I said. "We'll be right over." I hung up the phone.

"The dog's ready," I said to Vera.

She nodded. And the rest—you already know.

As any normal person would, I have gone over this scene again and again. Was there anything here strange or foreboding? I can only say that although I suspected she was unstable—there were, I see now, signs and signals—Vera was, very simply, virgin or no virgin, man or woman, the best lover I ever had.

The Missing Letter

I have kept all the letters Vera sent me and all the photographs her mother gave me in a folder entitled "Vera." They sit in my top desk drawer, untouched. I have not looked at them until now. But alas, the one fateful letter, the letter I raced in a Connecticut thunderstorm and through Kentucky bluegrass to retrieve—this letter I have lost. I may have left it in the writing cabin, for it is nowhere to be found. That was the last place I saw it. I will have to recount the contents of that letter to the best of my ability, then, and though you can trust me and I can trust myself to convey its essence, it is only in memory that it resides in toto and there—untouched—it is already given to eternity.

It began, as I recall, with an apology, and it ended with an apology, too.

"I'm sorry," it said, "I don't write you these last days." Or something to that effect.

Or perhaps it said, "I'm sorry I am distracted." Or, "I'm sorry, I love someone else."

Of course, she didn't say this last sentence until much later, as we know.

In the letter she said that Katya, her best friend in Russia, had run into "Yeh Yeh," the Russian initials of "linguistics professor," and had spoken to him. This was the man Vera had loved and left before she came to America. He had told Katya that in fact he was no longer married and had not been for a while, as Vera had thought, as he, presumably, had led her to believe, and that he'd had a child, a daughter, who had died at the age of six. It was this particular piece of information that affected Vera the most. It seemed, in fact, to undo her. She felt oddly responsible. The fact that she had left him without ever saying good-bye, that she had left the country, had disappeared, moreover, that he had no way to find her in the face of this news, tore her apart. "What should I do?" she asked. "He may think I too am dead." She felt guilty and responsible.

"I am sorry to write to you this letter," she said. "I feel so, so sorry." And then, for the first time, she signed her fax, "Love."

We spoke for a good three hours that night. I stood by the broad window of the writing cabin—a small one-room cottage deep in the woods behind my friend's barn—looking at my reflection through the dusty screen. Moths threw themselves against the wire from the gray darkness.

"Just tell me first," I said. "Are you leaving me?" The letter had a portentousness I couldn't explain. It seemed like a very convoluted first step out the door.

"No," she said.

"Okay, then. I'll tell you what's going on with me, then you tell me what's going on with you. Okay?"

"Yeah."

"I'm not interested in drama," I said. "And it sounds like you're leaving me. Why do you think there's something you have to do, and why were you so sorry to send me the letter?"

Vera didn't answer. She sighed deeply, again and again. I asked questions.

"Are you leaving me?"

"No."

"Did you send me that letter to test me?"

"Maybe," she said.

"Did you think it might upset me?"

"Yes. Maybe."

"Then why did you send it?"

Silence.

"You have to talk to me Vera. I can't just keep asking you questions. This is too important. I'm very upset. You're going to lose me if you can't speak to me and help me understand what's going on."

There was another sigh-laden silence.

"Vera?"

"Vera!"

"You're always so unsure," she burst out.

"About you?"

"Yes."

"Unsure of my love for you?"

"Yes."

"I love you more deeply than I've ever loved anyone else!" I found myself saying. I was beginning to get choked up. "I don't understand why you can't see that."

"You're always breaking up with me!" she cried.

"That's true. But I never mean it. Look, I always break up with everyone I love. Don't you think I know what it feels like when it feels different from what everything else felt like? I'm really in love with you, Vera!"

More heavy sighing.

"Can you believe me?"

Sigh.

"Do you believe me?"

Then she said, "How can I know you're still attracted to me?"

"Vera!"

Then there was a long, sexy silence. I listened to her breathing. I breathed and she breathed. We sat like that for a long time, breathing into the phone.

"I guess," she said, "you're answering that question every minute."

"What do you mean?"

"Every minute you talk to me you answer the question of whether or not you're attracted to me. It's not a one-minute question."

"Yes," I said softly. "That's right. It's true. Every minute I talk to you, I'm answering the question."

Then I lay on my back on the floor with a roll of paper towels under my head. We talked almost until morning. As light crept into the woods, I fell asleep on the window seat on my side.

July 3
Hi Babe!
The small package which I sent you today will be to you only in seven to ten days, it means, you'll receive it only after Russia, unfortunately.

Wish you again a wonderful trip, I miss you badly, am waiting you,
V-ka

July 8
I am sitting here, in San Francisco, and thinking of you, how you are there, in Russia. So strange. I didn't arrive to America in May, ninety-four, I am still living in my native city named Sankt-Petersburg, renamed several times. Petersburg-Petrograd-Leningrad-Petersburg. I am a student and go to college. It's night. It's my owl time. I am very nocturnal. In kitchen. Gas is turned on. Very blue light. It's very warm. Come to the window. Lantern and rare drunk walkers. Tomorrow will be a day.

I will go to crowded Nevsky. Didn't you see it in dreams several times? I don't have practice in English and I am very shy. I go to one of gay bars. Will I run into you? You are there, no doubt. You see in me something familiar and you are impressed. It even seems to you that you've met me somewhere.

Hallucination? Definitely, you know that we were very close. That we shared some night orchestrated by music and that it was in SF. Then we have conversation in Russian, in S. Petersburg. Then you come back to US. You feel unhappy you left me in Russia. You at your home. You hear: your phone is ringing. How nervous, without obvious reason, you are. Say hello. It's me. Let us meet. Who is that? Is it you? We meet and eat pizza. It's so strange. You say, I resembled you girl whom you met in Sankt-Pete. Is it a dream in your head? It seems that we spent some nights together in Russia. And I say: how happy I am that you came back to US.

V.

In my six weeks away from her, I received eleven faxes from Vera and sent sixteen. We spoke on the phone exactly twenty-one times.

Vera was very concerned I see where she came from, but most important was that I somehow connect with her life at the university, specifically "linguistics professor." One thing I need to emphasize: Vera gave me explicit directions about her city, and I followed. So I guess you could say, even before she was gone I was looking for her.

Petaluma

Many months later, I was in the car with a woman I had thought I could love. Her name was Melissa.

"In the last year I've dated seventeen women, kissed twelve, three of whom were ex-lovers, and slept with fourteen." I boasted.

"That's pretty impressive," Melissa said.

Even though what I told her was true, it embarrassed me that she was impressed, because I had been trying to impress her. She had been one of the girls I had kissed but hadn't slept with; I had met her in Boston. She was the first real girl after Vera—there was MLQ online, but being only a "virtual" girl, she doesn't quite count. For about twenty-four hours, I thought Melissa was it. I had really hoped it would work out. She was still in love with her old girlfriend Lola, though, or so she said, and needed "time."

"Oh, yeah," I said. "And I did a guy on the plane."

"What guy? What plane?" Melissa said.

"Oh, there was this guy sitting next to me. Actually, he was a really nice guy." I felt embarrassed, suddenly, to be telling her the story.

"So what happened?" Melissa asked. She was getting excited. "You did the guy on the plane? What does that mean?"

Melissa was into it, I could tell.

"You fucked him?"

"Not exactly."

"You let him fuck you?"

"Not exactly."

"Well, what did you do?"

"It's kind of a long story," I said.

"I'm all ears," Melissa said. I could tell she was having trouble driving. She was going really slowly, sitting right up against the steering wheel.

So I told her the story of Billie Blue in exquisite detail. Soon the windows of her Toyota were all fogged up. I kept seeing the same scrub oak by the same corral. We were going around in circles. She was concentrating so hard on my story that she really could hardly drive.

"You're wild," she kept saying.

"Yeah, but now it feels like forever since I've been touched," I replied. "The other day Alison put her hand on my shoulder and I jumped a mile."

"So did he come?" Melissa probed.

"All over the place," I said. "It was gross."

There was a silence then. A kind of sad and sexy silence rose up between us, perhaps a sorrow that nothing like this had happened between us.

"So, who was the last person you kissed?" Melissa asked.

We were finally heading out of Petaluma. I had finished telling her the story.

"I guess it was Vera," I said. "I slept with Vera the night after I got back, which was the night after Billie Blue. But, of course, that was pretty much the last time I saw her."

"Vera?"

"Yeah, Vera."

It was true, what I told Melissa, and yet for some reason it felt like a lie.

When I got home, Vita greeted me at the door, her bandy legs, beady eyes, and tight, excited snout all aquiver.

Don't think it didn't cross my mind to name this new pup Vera. It would, perhaps, have given me endless hours of amusement.

"Come, Vera. Sit, Vera," I might have said. "Vera, you stay right there." If you wanted to analyze it, you could say that in choosing Vita over Vera, I chose life over faith.

As for my Vera, the Vera, our one missing other: Fact is, I'm not even sure that was really her name.

The Escape Artist

Judith Katz

My dear Parents,

I am distressed to inform you that the wedding you planned for me is a figment of our sorry imaginations. Instead of experiencing a joyous celebration, I am a prisoner on this steamer, although I do not know for what reason I am held. After going to such great lengths (and expense) to woo me, Reb Goldenberg has abandoned me completely, and I believe his promise to marry me was a hoax. Who knows why he paid you all of those zloty? I am doubtful that I will ever see the fair city of Buenos Aires, for I am certain I will rot in this cabin, wither, and die. If he does not plan to marry me I cannot imagine what the "honorable" Tutsik Goldenberg plans to do with me.

Oh, woe is me! Rescue me if you can!

I remain,
Your daughter,
Sofia Teitelbaum

I folded my letter three times and wrote upon it the address in Poland of my mother and father. I placed it on my untouched dinner tray with the intention of asking the steward to mail it at his earliest opportunity. I lit another cigarette, poured myself just a bit more whiskey (for which I seemed to develop a taste almost immediately), and attempted to decipher the Spanish magazines.

I cannot tell you more about the hours that passed. I slept, woke, drank, slept again. Sometimes when I woke l looked at the newspaper and magazines, sometimes I peed into the pot, once or twice I ate some bites of food, two times I smoked a cigarette.

Then suddenly, in the midst of those furtive naps, the door to my cabin swung open with no knock preceding it, and at once I was surrounded by all three of them: *Tante* Sara, Dov Hirsh, and Tutsik Goldenberg. Each of them wore evening clothes, although Tutsik Goldenberg's were by far the fanciest. Sara looked bizarre, and when I saw her in her new clothes it took me a moment to know her. Her frumpy dress was gone, and now her skinny frame was draped in a shiny, spangled blue sheath, whose bodice was cut low as underwear and hung straight down to just above her knees. On her head she no longer had her flat straw hat but wore instead a single blue feather that curled around her face. It made her look no softer, no less severe. Dov Hirsh appeared to be a cheaply rendered version of Tutsik Goldenberg—his dinner jacket sleeves a bit too short, his black tie slipping over just a hair to the side. While Goldenberg's hair was brushed and oiled neatly, Hirsh's hung down over his face.

The three of them together frightened me. There was a sinister gleam in each set of eyes. I sat up on one elbow. A strap of my slip hung down over my shoulder. "So," I said, trying to hide my sleepiness, "the time has come at last for our wedding."

Tante Sara laughed. "My God, Tutsik, she's drunk!"

"Of course she's drunk, I sent her a bottle of whiskey." Tutsik Goldenberg proceeded to take the fine gold and diamond rings off his fingers one by one. He handed them to Hirsh without taking his eyes from my face. "I see my darling bride-to-be has made short work of it."

"Well, yes, it's frightfully boring here otherwise."

Tutsik waved a piece of writing paper in front of my face. "But you have managed to entertain yourself, it seems, by writing pleasant letters home."

"I don't know what you're talking about," I answered. My breath caught in my throat.

"Fortunately, I have a particularly good relationship with your steward. He made sure I saw this before it was sent off in the mail boat tomorrow." Without changing his stance or his demeanor, Tutsik Goldenberg, mild-mannered purveyor of imported jewels, lifted his hand and hit me with the flat of it full across my cheek. My face reverberated. Sara turned her head and put a finger into her mouth. Dov Hirsh smiled.

"You are never to write another letter like this one, do you understand?" He hit me again. "Under any circumstances, to anyone." A third blow followed. "Now, luckily for you, it is to my advantage to deliver you unmarked to our destination, which is indeed Buenos Aires." He snapped his immaculate fingers and Dov Hirsh dropped the rings into the palm of my groom-to-be's hand. One by one he replaced them. "I had hoped to avoid this, but for the rest of the journey, Sara will watch over you. I'd spell her with Hirsh, but he really can't be trusted. Pity—because of you, she will miss the fairest part of the journey." He held my ill-fated letter over my head and lit it with a match. Then he opened the porthole and threw the flaming paper out to sea.

I said nothing, only looked to Sara, then Dov Hirsh, then looked away. "Have another drink. The captain is a good friend of mine. He makes sure my guests and I are provided with only the best. Now then, Hirsh and I will go back to the dining room and finish our dinner. Sara is going to spend the night. Hopefully you and I will not speak again until we reach Argentina's rich and beautiful shore." He held me by the chin. "Is there anything else you would like, dear bride?"

To spit in your face, I thought, but I didn't say it. Really what I wanted more than anything was to be dead.

"Sara is an excellent pinochle player—it's rumored she's a sharp. Perhaps she'll teach you some of her fine tricks before the night is over." He touched his forehead and made as if to tip his hat. "*Buenas noches, Señorita*. Until we meet again."

We were alone together now, not in a coach, nor a compartment on a train, but here, in a tiny room aboard a boat steaming west. How I must have looked to her! My face smarting from Goldenberg's slaps, my eyes gleaming with tears. I covered myself as best I could, and still she stood before me, cold-eyed, her lips set in a smile that said to me nothing about happiness. She took her blue feather from around her face and kicked her shoes off.

She sat beside me on the bed. She leaned over me, touched

my cheek with the same finger she'd shoved in her mouth when Goldenberg hit me, then drew it down over my lips, under my chin, traced my shoulders and the edge of my slip. Then without a word Sara kissed me, pushed my lips open with her tongue, and sucked her way into me.

I was horrified and held my breath, did not move a muscle. Yet when she put both hands under my behind and pulled me to her, pushed my thighs apart and pressed her knee between my legs, some place inside of me felt a horrible thrill. She held me in this way for what seemed forever, kissing, holding, pressing. I was on fire and devoured all at once.

She stood up and moved the straps of her beaded dress over her shoulders. It slipped to the floor and landed at her ankles in a glittery mound. And there she was, Tutsik Goldenberg's ersatz *Tante* Sara, naked before me. She leaned over and kissed me again; her breasts brushed my own. I squirmed to get away from her, and I gasped with strange pleasure. "Are you really Tutsik Goldenberg's aunt?" I whispered.

She burst out in a single laugh, then purred, "*Momentito.*" I lay completely still as she moved quickly to the cabin door and made certain it was locked. She came and lay beside me on the bed and kissed me once again.

Was it the whiskey? Was it the flat boredom of my captivity? Or had she tapped my most secret desire? How could I know what I was even meant to do? Somehow, I was brave then. I felt Sara's mouth on my own, I felt her hands on my breasts and behind, and soon my lips became greedy for hers, and I was feverish and full of what I cannot tell you. I was swept away. Sara said nothing but certainly was not silent.

She knew far better than I how kissing was done and was much more expert at it than that wondrous Tamar, my childhood friend. She knew how to make me move my fingers and hands to secret places without saying a word. She held me about the hips and waist, burrowed into me with her fingers and face, encouraged me to do the same to her. I was fearful but very wild. I was hungry and hot and dangerous. I had felt nothing like this in my entire life. Was this what Tamar had wanted from me and I from her? It didn't matter now, for having once tasted such a meal as this, I would hunger for it the rest of my life.

How much time passed I never knew. When we stopped, Sara looked past me and suddenly sat up. She lit a cigarette and poured out two whiskeys. I tried to kiss her on the mouth again, but she wouldn't let me. Instead she handed me a glass. "Drink this," she commanded, and I obeyed.

I gulped down the whiskey. How it burned in my throat, how it opened up in the back of my head. I put down my glass and she poured me another. "You'll have no problem when we get to Talcahuano Street. Just do for Perle what you did for me. You'll have it soft until you turn twenty, yes, you'll have it soft. This I guarantee."

I didn't know what she was talking about, but I couldn't ask. I just looked at her as she sat beside me. Sara, whose eyes were dead, whose jaw was tight and set against everything, and yet who with just her hands, her mouth and tongue, had made me into a wild beast. Sara, with sallow skin and crooked teeth, stubby little fingers that looked nothing like the rest of her, who took long pulls of whiskey, not out of a glass but straight from the bottle. Who moments ago (was it only moments?) had had

me in her arms and at her mercy, had taken me at last from this
tiny locked room into what village, what country, I had no idea.
And now she said nothing, just stared past me to the porthole.
"Not bad, little bride. No, not bad."

I dreamed again of my Polish home, my mother in a bride's
dress, me naked and laughing. She carried me on her shoulders
down a muddy street, brought me house to house, knocked on
every door. No one answered until the butcher's wife stood with
her hands on her hips in the doorway. "You're late," she said,
and *tsked*. "Late for the wedding, late for Tamar!"

"Too late for Tamar?" my mother asked.

"Too late for Tamar?" My own heart sank.

But there she stood, behind the butcher, my childhood neighbor,
my girlhood friend, lovely Tamar. Tamar in her own wedding
dress, her lush, red hair flying about her every which way.
And here another miracle occurred, another miracle of Tamar—
who lived in the flat beneath mine and saw my soul, who sat
beside me in history class, who looked over my shoulder in
chemistry—sweetest Tamar, my childish love, who just one time
bestowed on me a frantic kiss. Ah, Tamar, finally, in this dream,
on this day, in a beautiful bride's dress with hair that could burn,
delivered at last by my own mother's hand. I picked her up from
behind that butcher, took her into my own arms, and kissed her
myself at last.

And I woke then with a horrible start, to the stuffy cabin and
Sara's thin back. It was still and gray; I could barely breathe. I
stared into the darkness and wept. I wept and I wondered if that
wasn't why they did it: if my parents hadn't sold me out for a few

zloty because somehow or other they knew that in my heart of hearts it was a woman I wanted.

I did not come off the ship as others did, to warm arms and comforting friends. I was wheeled off the boat, down the gang-plank, in a wooden chair, bundled in blankets and shawls with an old straw hat such as Sara wore when first we met, in her *Tante* Sara disguise. It was she who did the pushing, no longer that hot, brittle Sara whose cold kisses kept me quiet the long rest of our journey, but *Tante* Sara, in those old same *Tante* Sara clothes. As she pushed she spoke to me in a birdlike, soothing Yiddish, which I barely remember because I was drugged. They put something in my whiskey and something in the food and this, mixed with the aftermath of Sara's long kisses, guaranteed I wouldn't make trouble now. Who showed my papers, who carried my bags, I do not know. I was gone. All I remember is the *bumpity-bump* of the chair on the gangplank, a certain crush of people in all directions at once. Then the *bump bump bump* over cobblestones on our way to my new home.

I know now there were people on the docks that day looking out for the likes of me. Looking out for young women with men who smelled like Tutsik Goldenberg, or young girls with no one who were greeted by flashy aunts or uncles who looked like Dov Hirsh, with cruel-as-ice glints in their eyes. These watchers were from the Jewish Ladies Protection Society. They were making sure that ones such as I could be rescued from fates such as mine. But Perle Goldenberg and her brother Tutsik were wise to their kindness. Long ago they had learned to take pre-cautions. So here I was, no longer a drugged and terrified sixteen-year-old fresh from Warsaw, just off the boat. I was transformed into another *tante*, *Tante* Sofia, my lover Sara's decrepit old aunt. From Lodz, not Warsaw, an aunt, not a mark, as old as a woman can be.

I've seen it since. I know how they worked it. Rolled me past those watchful Protection Society eyes, past those dear women with their notebooks and photographs of Red Ruthie and Madam Perle. They rolled me past the police who couldn't care less, and the soldiers whom I would one day service, until we were in the clear. Then they lifted me into a *droshky*, Sara jumped in beside me, and we were on our way to Talcahuano Street, my new home.

Was it raining? It was May, so maybe it was. It was likely damp and chill, but who remembers? Maybe it was a wonderful day, a rare winter thing in Buenos Aires. Yes, perhaps the sky was blue and clear and only a damp breeze blew down cobbled streets. It didn't matter, for after I was carted to my new home in Talcahuano Street I was trundled up a narrow flight of stairs and brought up to bed. I was allowed to sleep then, but for how many days I don't know. When I woke again it was indeed raining. I found myself in a satin camisole with Sara beside me on the bed. She was transformed, once again, in an open kimono, nothing underneath, smiling that joyless smile. She held a hollow gourd painted black, with a silver-tipped straw in it. "Drink this, my darling." She offered it with no warmth, but her eyes seemed just a bit softer. "Revive yourself, for soon our dear mistress is coming to call."

I sipped from the straw, although reluctantly. I knew that the drugs they gave me on the boat were in me still. But when Sara touched my cheek and kissed me on the neck I fell to her, in spite of myself. All she desired I would provide, anything she asked at all. And so I sipped from the silver straw, my first real taste of Argentina, in a locked room with slats for windows and a high ceiling and sad dreams to come.

"This is how we drink tea here in Argentina," said dead-faced Sara. She touched my cheek. My breath caught. "It's called mate."

"But where am I drinking it?" I asked, in a horrible panic, "and where are my clothes?"

Sara shook her head and pulled away. "You're home, little sister, dear cousin and niece. Welcome home now, dear auntie and lover. Madam Perle will appear in a minute or two, and your life in this world will start over. But remember," she whispered, "Madam Perle may not look like one of those prim ladies who sits in the balcony at shul every chance she gets, but in truth, she is pious and sees herself as one of the righteous. No matter how you are tempted, do not, under any circumstances, take God's name—or Madam Perle's for that matter—in vain."

The door of my tiny room swung open, and there before me, framed in that window of garish bordello light, stood the queen of Talcahuano Street, the woman now in charge of my fate, my new mother, Madam Perle.

Tutsik Goldenberg's sister was an astonishing beauty. Even in my stupor I could see this, and, indeed, it was nearly impossible to reconcile the way she looked at that moment with what Sara told me. She wore a fabulous green dressing gown over a black corselet, silk stockings, and open-toed satin slippers. Her luxurious black hair was piled atop her head, and two heavy gold hoops dangled from her ears. Her face was painted. I had never seen such a face. Her lips were scarlet, there were thick black lines across her eyelids, and her lashes were long and lush. She wore rows of bracelets on each arm; when she moved her hands to speak they made a soothing jingle. Unlike her brother Tutsik, this woman, this Perle Goldenberg, exuded a remarkable, a breath-taking warmth. And yet, if one looked closely into those black eyes of hers, there was something of a madwoman there, something a person saw from time to time if she looked into the eyes of those women in the Warsaw marketplace who had a fish in one hand and a prayer book in the other.

She sat on the bed beside me. She smelled like lilacs and roses. She took my chin between her fingers and made soothing sounds. "How do you feel, sweet Sofia? Still a little groggy, eh?" She patted my cheek gently and cooed, "I'm so sorry about the drugs, darling. It's best to calm you down before you meet the authorities. They can't ask you questions if you're asleep, and after such a long trip...well, who wants to be bothered." She gave my hand a little squeeze. "Sara here has shown you some of the ropes, I understand. There are a few more things you'll need to know before we can call it work, eh? Come to my rooms tomorrow when you're rested and I'll explain everything. Are you hungry, *neshomeleh?*"

In truth, I felt faint and famished, but I was afraid to say.

"Oh, I am certain," Perle clucked over me like a mother hen, "I am certain you are starving after that long boat ride, and for a good Polish meal, I'll bet. The food on board ship is appalling, my dear. We'll have Marianna bring you up a lovely meal. Why, just this minute she is cooking a delectable cabbage *borscht*. If word gets out, the entire Jewish community will be banging on our door for dinner. Yes, *borscht*, black bread, a little sour cream. You'll be back on your feet in no time. But that's not really where we want you, is it." She chuckled softly. Unlike when Dov Hirsh laughed, it was clear to me that I was meant to be in on the joke, not the brunt of it. I wasn't sure why it was funny, but in spite of myself, I giggled, too.

Sara whispered something in Spanish to Perle. "Ah," Madam Perle nodded her head and once again touched my face. "Sara tells me you have been concerned about your things—a valise, she tells me, and a cardboard box?"

"Yes, those, and a pair of silver candlesticks." It was the first I had spoken in a long while, and my voice shook.

Perle looked at me sadly. "I'm afraid the candlesticks are nowhere to be found, my dear. But don't despair. The Sabbath is strictly observed in this house, and you may say the blessings over our candles every Friday night if you like. As to your other luggage, it's all right here in this room." She snapped her fingers and Sara put the wedding dress box in my lap.

"There," pronounced Madam Perle brightly, "just like Chanukah."

That was the moment my heart broke in Buenos Aires, once and for all. Was it the loss of the candlesticks, or the thought of my practical joke wedding dress? To this day I can't tell you. In spite of myself, I burst into tears.

"Oh, little *ziskeit*." Perle took the box from me and slipped it under the bed. She touched my cheek, and I cried even louder. "Ah." She leaned over and kissed me sweetly on the forehead. "I know what you're going through, Sofia. Sea travel always makes me melancholy, too. We'll leave you here to your dreams now," she crooned. "You must try, darling, not to be sad."

If I did have dreams that night, they were full of men with straight razors and women with knitting needles chasing me about the streets of Warsaw. I didn't have much time to remember them or think about their meaning, for I was summoned by Perle the very next day. Thoughts of my time with her were meant to occupy both my waking and my sleeping life.

It was Sara who came to get me. She held out a blue silk wrapper. "Put this on. Courtesy of the house," she said flatly. "First we give you a bath, then you have an appointment with her Holiness, the boss." Sara sneered when she said this, and my heart stopped, but I followed her down the hall to a room with a big claw-foot tub, which was already full of steaming, perfumed water. Sara took my robe and watched as I reluctantly stepped in. "Go ahead, Sofia, think of it this way—it's your own private *mikveh*. Then you go get blessed."

I sank down and let the water play against my chin. I am sorry to say that after all the hotel rooms and my life on the ship, the bath water felt miraculous.

Sara handed me a huge round sponge and a bar of rose-colored soap. "Scrub yourself good, and don't get too comfy. Madam wants to see you in half an hour." She turned then and walked away.

I had never had such a bath in my life, in that big long tub with water that came from a tap already hot. I splashed about and rubbed soap all over me—wonderful, flowery soap. I laughed and thought, *This isn't so bad, a bath like this and a robe like that.* Then Sara came back and rubbed me dry with a towel as big as I was, the way my mother used to when I was a little girl. I started to cry then, but I held the tears back. I didn't want anybody to know what a dope, what a baby, what a fool I was. How could my parents have let me go?

Once I was dried and perfumed, hair brushed and tied, Sara brought me at last to Perle's rooms down the hall. She knocked and a velvet voice said, "Come, darling." Sara nodded, and I walked in alone.

There were candles burning in Perle's room, although it was 3:00 in the afternoon. Incense smoldered, as sweet, mysterious music spilled softly from a gramophone. Now, my room here had a bed that could easily hold two; Perle Goldenberg's bed could hold four. On my first visit to Madam Perle, at least a dozen pillows lay against that headboard, each covered with a satin case. Spread across the bed was a pink coverlet, and under this coverlet, propped up against those many pillows, sat a radiant Madam Perle.

She wore a robe that matched her sheets, and her hair was on top of her head in a swirl. She was reading a book by candlelight, sipping her tea through a straw. She put her book down, pushed back the covers, and said, "Come sweetheart, come sit by me."

Now you may wonder, with all the education Sara provided me on the good ship *Viktorius* as we steamed across the ocean, what was left for Madam Perle to teach. And it is true that thanks to icy Sara, by the time Perle invited me into her enormous bed I was already wise to some of the reluctant pleasures of my own body. But Madam Perle put me wise to the fact that my desire, or my *seeming* desire, could bring passion and yearning to others. She also did what Sara would never do in a million centuries: with each trick of my new trade, Madam Perle provided little homilies and fairy tales about how good these acts would get me in with God.

"I kiss you so."

She did, an exquisite kiss that pulled me into her, that melted me on the spot. Even as I tried to protest I moaned. "Ah, you're a natural, Sofia. In this line of work, your job is to do exactly as you've done—respond! Tell the truth—you felt that kiss, you liked it; isn't it so? But remember, dolly, as our very own Bible tells us, it is better by far to give than to receive. Pleasure in this house is a job, dear, but done properly, it will bring you many blessings. Why, just listen to the men when you have them in the throes of ecstasy. Some will curse you, it's true, but most, when the job's well done, will call upon the Lord above to bless you and keep you. And some, so satisfied, so transfixed by their pleasure, will even call out the lord God's name. Don't be shocked when this happens, and don't relinquish yourself to that ecstasy, either. Now"—she laid upon my lips a second, most extraordinary kiss— "you like that. I can tell. But if you let go and relax too much, your life here will soon turn to hell. Respond if you must, but hold back your heart. Show feeling, but don't feel too much. When a man puts his fingers all over you, seem pliant, but don't give in to his touch. It's hard not to succumb to my caress. I'm irresistible, I know. But with men—it's easy, trust me. You'll see. Stay in control and you'll be in control, you'll be queen of the world. Look at me.

"When a man is panting and pushing, pumping on top of you and calling out to God, calling you his sweetest dear," she rolled her eyes back in her head and started writhing on the bed, "your job is to act as if he were the world's most marvelous lover, to call him by his first name, or better yet his private one, to melt under him, to make him think he is the world to you—and never to feel a thing."

On that cursed ship *Viktorius*, Sara had brought out the vildeh in me, the wild animal. Here in the Talcahuano Street *shandhoiz*, Madam Perle went on to show me how to bring out the *vildeh* in others. She continued to lecture me on what customers would demand, and how they would demand it, drawing upon her vast experience. "You shall do as they ask, Sofia, for in spite of what dry old rabbis tell us, the Talmud prescribes pleasure, and pleasure you must provide! Think of yourself as an ancient handmaiden."

Madam Perle drew my horrified attention to a dazzling vial of golden oil. "They will ask you," she told me, as we lay in that enormous bed, "to anoint their precious *shvontzes*, and then order you to suck them off. Be sure to use only the oils we keep in the *shandhoiz*, nothing else. Sometimes these mangoes bring their own oil. It's frequently poison and makes the mouth swell shut. Take their vial, make as if you're using it, but distract them. Tell them what a sacred scepter that *shlang* of theirs is and then replace the oil with ours. If you have trouble putting that thing in your mouth, remember again, the Torah commands pleasure. You may find this particular form of it disgusting at first, but you'll get used to it after a while. They like you to swallow their semen. My advice in this case is to act like you've done it, then spit it out discreetly. Have you ever seen a man take his penis into his own hands and make himself come? I'm certain you have, for they do it on the streets of Warsaw all the time. It's a comical, pitiful sight. They become even more grotesque than they normally are. And those poor *shlubs* are spilling their seed! There's no hope for them in heaven. Just remember this and you'll always be in control. *Farshtais?*"

She passed me her *mate*. I took a sip, but my throat was tight from all this talk of sucking men. I swallowed, finally; she smiled. She pinched my cheek, she touched my hair. "*Neshomeleh*, sweetheart...so much like I was at your age."

Then Perle handed me that vial of amber-colored liquid. "Put a drop here," she said, pointing to her lovely rouged nipple. I was terrified to touch her. "Just a drop on the finger." She tipped the bottle onto her own finger and held it under my nose. "Lovely, eh?" She rubbed the oil onto my nipple. I caught my breath. It was as if my breast were suddenly on fire, and yet it felt almost good. Madam Perle chuckled and kissed me on the top of my head. "Nice, isn't it?" She handed me the vial. "Now, anoint me. Make me feel holy, too."

I did as I was told and placed a tiny amount on the tip of Perle's breast. She lay back and sighed luxuriously. "Wonderful, Sofia. Now drip the oil into the palms of your hands and hold it there until it warms. Just a few seconds. Rub your hands together lightly if you like...good...now spread the oil out across my belly and slowly work your hands down to my *peeric*." She pointed to her vagina but did not touch herself. "Come ahead, I won't bite. Though if I do, it wouldn't be so bad."

I took a breath and gingerly rubbed the oil over Madam's soft, round belly, then down toward the line of her pubic hair, which was black and silky and, to my surprise—and I'll admit it, delight—woven into a tiny braid that was tied with a thin lavender ribbon just at its tip.

Madam whispered from deep in her throat, "Now stick your finger into me."

I held my breath and pushed my forefinger into her vagina, which was very wet and warm.

"Now, quick," she murmured, at the edge of her breath, "take it away."

I pulled my finger out. Madam Perle groaned. She reached over and held my face in her hands. "You're a quick study, *hartseniu*. Oh, you'll do very nicely...now kiss me."

I cleared my throat and went for her lips. She stopped me with the palm of her hand. "I told you to kiss me and I meant it, but not on the mouth. Darling, kiss me down here."

In the days that followed, Madam Perle taught me much about the business of sexual pleasure and all things that accompanied it. She showed me how to smoke cigars and informed me which ones the great rabbis of Poland preferred. She explained which type of drinking alcohol was best in winter and which in summer, which ones the Talmud suggested, and which ones a woman could get away with sipping all day long.

Deftly she demonstrated the various tools of our whore trade. She showed me the many uses of the feather boa, the silk robe, the satin sheet and velvet quilt, and she explained the possible religious implications of each. In the privacy of her rooms, Madam instructed me in the ways to employ a leather cock, showed me how to tie a man down with silk scarves, demonstrated how I might ride him like a horse or offer my ass up to him like a dog. She taught me which great scholar enjoyed which implements and positions.

Sometimes these lessons disgusted me; other times I was fascinated. Sara contended that Madam Perle made up these stories as she went along, but I'm not so certain.

There was a part of Madam's teachings—including the ways in which a lady must hold a blackjack to get the best results when she wished to leave a gentleman knocked out cold; the fastest way to remove a wallet full of pesos from the vest pocket of a well-dressed dandy and put it back again, minus the pesos; the surest spot to place a knife blade when you want an irritating gentleman to please leave you alone ("trust me, Sofia, it ain't against the jugular")—that I found intriguing. "If he tries to beat you, if he flashes a razor, even if he has a gun, call out and Tutsik or Hirsh will come get him, for no man in this house is allowed to strike a woman." That was what I was told.

Good *morah* that she was, Perle sweetened my studious excellence with rewards: special delights for my pleasure only, demonstrations of her world-renowned tricky dexterity with hands and tongue, which included her ability to have fingers in three, four, or five places at once and still leave me begging for more.

But for me, her favors in bed and her peculiar interpretations of the Tanuch and the Talmud were the least of it. For the walls of Perle Goldenberg's bedroom were covered from floor to ceiling with books, many of which she found useful when instructing me in the art of my new vocation. Others had nothing to do with sex or God at all; they were simply wonderful stories. Madam Perle handed me Yiddish translations of French novels; read aloud verses by the Greek poet Sappho; lay beside me, belly down on the bed, and paged with me through picture books from Japan and Constantinople containing drawing upon drawing of women with legs spread and men with penises hard, dressed and naked, wrestling with each other in positions so complicated and so many that soon they engendered in me only boredom. There was also on those shelves a sorry reminder of home, for Tutsik Goldenberg had purchased my father's leather-bound Shakespeare, and on my third day of lessons, how it startled me to see it by her bed. I said nothing and she said nothing, simply slipped the book under a pillow and motioned me, *Come ahead.*

In those earliest days when she called me to her, I did not know if I should simply enjoy her kisses, the feel of her tongue on my nipples and ass, all clearly designed to thrill me, or believe her when she said that God looked down and saw a *mitzvah* where I saw horrible pleasure. As if reading my mind, she'd whisper in that breathtaking way, "Be grateful, Sofia; this life is blessed and golden. Many look down upon us, but as I have told you many times, this profession is a gift from God. From the earliest days of the holy temple we women of pleasure have always been its guardians. Take this charge seriously, and your work here will be a journey of spirit that will bring you closer to heaven.

"Besides," Perle continued, "Tutsik has saved you from much worse fates."

For the first time since my ordeal began I almost laughed. Perle took my face between her fingers and was not gentle. "Would you rather be breaking your back in a sweatshop working for two or three pennies a day? Here you get the

Shabbes off, eat good kosher meals, and are strongly encouraged to pray."

I didn't know what to answer. For at least in a sweatshop at the end of the day a person might leave and walk home in the open air. True, on Friday nights, Marianna brought me a most delicious portion of chicken, and a strange hush filled the whorehouse walls. I was pampered in a joyless way, though, with chocolates and fancy perfumes, and except for her books, and her promise of God, I was leery of pleasures in Perle Goldenberg's rooms.

Esther's Story

Joan Nestle

I had heard of Esther. She was tough, a *passing* woman whose lover was a prostitute. Sea Colony talk. We all knew stories about one another, but like huge ice floes, we could occupy the same ocean without touching. This night we touched. She was sitting at the bar speaking a soft Spanish to Maria, the bartender from Barcelona. Amid the noise and smoke, Esther sat straight and still, a small, slim woman who dressed butch. Her profile was severe, gray hair rising from her forehead and waving back in the classic DA style. A small mole broke the tautness of her face. I do not remember how our contact began, but at some point I was standing between her legs as she sat with the lights of the bar at her back. Her knees jutted out around me like a sharp cove on a rocky shore. She joked with me, and I worried that I could not hold her attention. I was not sure I wanted to. We were wary of each other, but an erotic need had flashed between us, and neither of us would let it go.

Later that night she offered to take me home. We agreed to

go for a drive first. The night was dark, and Esther drove with ease, one hand on the wheel, the other holding her endless cigarette. She told me how she had left Ponce, Puerto Rico, her grown sons, and her merchant sailor husband to come to America to live like she wanted. Her family had cursed her, and she had built a new family here in New York. Her life was hard. Her girlfriend gave her a lot of trouble; they both had struggled with drugs, but life was getting better now. She enjoyed driving the taxi, and because her customers thought she was a man, they never bothered her. I looked at her, at the woman in a neat white shirt and gray pants, and wondered how her passengers could be so deceived. It was our womanness that rode with us in the car, that filled the night with tense possibilities.

Our ride ended in a vast parking lot at Jones Beach. Spotted around the lot were other cars, far enough away from one another so that lovers could have privacy. We sat in silence for a while, with Esther's cigarette a sharp red circle moving in the car's darkness. She put out the light and turned toward me. I leaned into her, fearing her knowledge, her toughness—and then I realized her hands were trembling. Through my blouse, I could feel her hands like butterflies shaking with respect and need. Younger lovers had been harder, more toughened to the joy of touch, but my passing woman trembled with her gentleness. I opened to her, wanting to wrap my fuller body around her leanness. She was pared down for battle, but in the privacy of our passion she was soft and careful. We kissed for a long time. I pressed my breasts hard into her, wanting her to know that even though I was young, I knew the strength of our need, that I was swollen with it. Finally she pulled away, and we started the long drive home. She asked me if she could spend the night. I said no, because I had to get up to go to work in a couple of hours and because I could no longer balance my need for Esther and the fear that I was beginning something I could not control. She said she would call. She told me later that I was the first woman who had said no to her. She said it with admiration, and I felt dishonest. It was not femme purity that kept me from her that night.

A few weeks passed, and I was sitting in the back room of the Sea Colony waiting for Vicki to return from cruising in the front room. A Seven-and-Seven appeared on the table. "Compliments of her," the waitress said, gesturing to the corner. I turned to see Esther smile, constrained but amused. Later in the night, when all things were foggier, I heard a whisper in my ear, "You will be mine." I just saw the shadow of her face before she disappeared.

She called not long after, and I invited her to dinner. I knew I was testing my boundaries, and I think she was, too. I was a young femme seeking the response of women I adored, needing their desire deep inside of me. I had brought several women home to my railroad apartment on East Ninth Street, but usually I was in control: I was sexually more expressive and on my own territory. From the first with Esther, I knew it would be different. I was twenty, and she was forty-five. I had been out only two years, and she had already lived lifetimes as a freak. Her sexuality was a world of developed caring, and she had paid a dear price for daring to be as clearly defined as she was.

The day of our dinner dragged at work. I knew I would not have time to change from work clothes and cook dinner before she arrived. At least that was my excuse for staying in my heels, nylons, and dress. But the deeper reason was that I wanted her to see my competent femme self, self-supporting and sturdy, and then I wanted her to reach under my dress, to penetrate the disguise I wore in a world that saw me as having no sexuality because I had neither boyfriend nor husband.

I bought a steak and mushrooms on the way home, prepared a big salad, and set the oval table in the third room, the combined living room and bedroom. This was a scene I had prepared many times before, my foreplay of giving. Each time I had felt fear and pride that two women could dare each other so. At 7:30 she knocked. I opened the door breathlessly, as if I had run a long way. She walked past me and stood in the center of the living room, looking around, while I explained that I had not had time to change. She was wearing a white-on-white shirt with ruffles down the front, sharply creased black pants, and loafers. Her slimness shone clean and sharp. All of a sudden I felt everything in the apartment was too big: I was too big, the table was too full, my need was too big. Esther stood quietly, looking at the set table filled with my offerings.

"Can't I do something for you, please?" she said. She examined the old apartment until she found a chair that needed fixing. "I'll fix that for you."

"No, no, please, you don't have to."

"I want to."

She left and returned in a few minutes with some tools. She turned the chair upside-down and repaired it. Only then would she allow herself to sit at my table. "So much food." We both ate very little, weighed down by the erotic tension in the room.

After dinner I asked if she would mind if I took a bath. Since

I had started working at age thirteen, I'd had a need to separate the workday from my own time by taking a bath. The hot water marked the border between my world and theirs. Tonight there was another reason as well: I knew we were going to make love, and I wanted to be clean for her. Since my tub was in the kitchen and there were no doors between the rooms, it meant she could watch as I bathed. She did not. When I finished, I put on a robe and went to sit next to her. Joan Baez played on the phonograph, and we spoke half in English, half in Spanish about our lives. She asked me about my job, school; I asked her about her girlfriend, driving the taxi.

The room was dark. We always met in darkness, it seemed. I knew that soon she would touch me, and I was already wet with wanting her. Here, now, on the bed, all the offerings would be tested. We both had power in our hands. She could turn from me and leave me with my wetness, my need—a vulnerability and a burden. I could close up, turn away from her caring and her expertise. But neither happened. With extreme tenderness, she laid me down. We kissed for a few minutes, and soon her hands knew I was not afraid. She smiled above me. "I know why you took that bath, to be clean for me." We began caring but demanding lovemaking. As I rose to her, she said, "*Dámelo, Juanita, dámelo.*" I strained to take and give to her, to pour my wetness in gratitude upon her hands and lips. But another part of me was not moving. I was trying so hard to be good for her, to respond equally to her fullness of giving, that I could not come. She reached for pillows and put them under my hips. My legs opened wider. I held Esther's head in my hands as her tongue and fingers took my wetness and my need. I had never felt so beautiful. She reached deep into me, past the place of coming, into the center of my womanness. But I could do no more. I put my hand over her lips and drew her up along my body.

"Please, no more. It feels wonderful, and you have given me deep, deep pleasure."

"Come home with me, I have things that will help."

I knew she meant a dildo, and I wanted her to know it was not a lack of skill or excitement that was stopping me. It was her forty-five years of wisdom, her seriousness, her commitment to herself, and now her promising of it to me, that scared me. She lay still beside me; only her slenderness made lying on that small bed possible. I turned to touch her, but she took my hand away from her breast. "Be a good girl," she said. I knew I would have to work many months before Esther would allow me to find her wetness as she had found mine. The words, the language of my people, floated through my head—*untouchable, stone butch.* Yet it was Esther who lay beside me, a woman who trembled when she held me. Before she left she told me if I ever needed to reach her in the afternoons, she'd be next door sitting with an old woman, *una vieja,* a woman she had known for years who was now alone. She gave me the woman's number.

The next day was Saturday, and I spent the morning worrying about what I had done, my failure to perform. One-night stands are not simple events: sometimes in that risk taking a world is born. I was washing my hair in the sink when I heard a knock at the door. Expecting a friend, I draped the towel around my naked shoulders and opened the door to an astonished delivery man. He thrust a long white box toward me as he turned his head. I took the box and closed the door. I had never had a messenger bring me a gift before. Twelve red roses lay elegantly wrapped in white tissue paper, a small square card snuggled between the stems:

Gracias, por todo anoche,
De quien te puede amar profundamente
Y con sinceridad—Esther

For one moment the Lower East Side was transformed for me: unheard-of elegance, a touch of silk had entered my life. Esther's final gift. We never shared another night together. Sometimes I would be walking to work and would hear the beeping of a horn. There would be Esther rounding the corner in her cab with her passenger who thought she was a man.

Act of Creation

Clara Thaler

For the first eighteen summers of her life, my mother, Sosha, left her tiny apartment in Brooklyn and came to this town, nestled like a jewel in the curve of the Connecticut coastline, to her grandparents' house, perched like a squat gull on a hill, overlooking the sound. When she was younger, six or seven, too small to walk down to the beach by herself, she would find refuge from the sweltering humidity under the kitchen table. The fringed tablecloth filtered the light, letting in the voices of her ma, her bubbe, and her bubbe's friends, as they prepared dinner or played endless games of rummy. Their voices were hushed, conspiratorial, often broken by a sudden burst of laughter: Sosha's bubbe and her friends knew all the secrets about the women in the town whose stomachs grew big only a month or two after their weddings, about the husbands who did not come home after work but drove to other towns to meet other women. "*Az der putz shtayt, der sachel gayt,*" Bubbe would conclude, and the women's laughter, muffled by the tabletop, would fill my mother's ears. It was in those sticky summers that she learned Yiddish, piecing together words, learning from the context and the women's voices. One story my mother puzzled over for weeks: A distant aunt, Sadie, had apparently gotten married with the hopes of raising a large family. But something had gone wrong with her husband, Hy; according to Sosha's bubbe, *"Nisht gkent zien a mensch."* As the years passed, Sadie grew despondent, until she died of a*"tzubruchena hartz."*My mother was mystified: what prevented Hy from being a *mensch?* She thought she must have missed a word, a phrase that would have explained it.

Years later, I learned Yiddish at the same kitchen table, after my grandmother died and my mother moved into the beachside house with my brother, Ari, and me. My father, who was already engaged to a shiksa from Manhattan and who had helped us load the moving truck, moved into a small apartment in Bayside. Ma's conversation was heavily peppered with Yiddish words, and when I was fifteen I begged her to write down some phrases for me to study and learn. *"Vos mach stu?"* I read from the notes my mother had given me, then repeated, "How are you?" Ma took to calling me *ketzi,* short for *ketzeleh,* kitten. The language reminded me of the house we lived in: weathered, full of warmth, deeply rooted in the past.

Now I live here alone. Ari moved to Los Angeles last spring, leaving me his golden retriever, Samson; Ma has taken a small ground-floor apartment a few towns down the shoreline, where there are no steps to trouble her arthritic legs. The house has been passed down to me, as a reward for having finally earned my master's degree in studio art, after years of false starts and faltering resolve.

It has been a month since Naomi moved out. It is springtime, but the house feels barren, dark.

I called her last week, at her sister's, where I thought she might have been staying; but the line was busy. I wondered if the phone was off the hook. I wondered if Naomi was there, maybe with another woman, maybe someone she met at one of the bars she likes in Manhattan. The thought is cruel, masochistic. My imagination is sharp and pricks me like a needle.

I met Naomi at a tiny gallery opening, downtown; her father was the gallery's owner, and a few of my sculptures were being shown. She was drunk, came over and introduced herself, then pulled me outside, near the shrubbery behind the building, and delivered a scathing (if desultory) condemnation of the gallery, her father, and art in general. She was twenty-two. I was twenty-nine, three semesters away from finishing my degree. Naomi demanded I drive her home; it wasn't until I pulled into her driveway that she asked me what I was studying. She apologized profusely, and again the next evening, over coffee. Three months later she moved in.

I am in the kitchen, rinsing my supper dishes in the sink. It is early evening, the sun beginning its slow descent. I make the water warmer, hold the plate under the tap, let the water pressure push bits of food off of the ceramic and into the drain. I rub at the forks with my fingertips, pressing the tines into the pad of my thumb. Samson is hungry. Naomi read somewhere that a raw egg mixed in with the dog's food will make his fur shinier; Samson now refuses to eat his meals un-egged. I take his bowl and a can of dog food from the cabinet, open the refrigerator. Samson's tail thumps expectantly on the floor, once, twice.

I crack the egg against the side of Samson's bowl, press my thumbs into the fissure, and spread the two halves of the shell. The jelly-whiteness that slides into the bowl contains two yolks. "Twins," I say aloud, to no one.

Naomi loved this house immediately, had considered it a sign of something worthwhile in me that I had not attempted sweeping repairs: its white paint is peeling, showing the dark wood underneath; the brick steps leading up to the front door are gap-toothed, and some of the slate-gray shutters hang crookedly. Inside, the angles of the living room are surprising and asymmetrical. But, upstairs, on the cramped second floor, is a view from the arched bedroom window that made Naomi and me forgive the architect's whimsy: the sound lies spread before the house, a glittering mirror of the sky, and every night the water catches and holds the colors of the sunset so that it seems the sound itself is pink, and blue, and orange.

Samson finishes his egg-and-dog-food and scratches at the back door. I hook the leash to his collar and let the door bang shut behind us. It has been thirty-two days since I came home after class to find a letter on the kitchen table. I read it once, then again. Hours later I burned my hand, badly, on the stove.

Naomi had written of the wisdom of not rushing into something too serious, of her fear in the face of strong emotions. I put the letter away in a drawer. As the weeks pass, her vague request for more time has begun to haunt me-I have stilled the pendulum of the hallway clock to silence its ticking. I take walks and come home to silence.

Samson, like all his breed, loves the water. I walk him up the shoreline, and he snuffles at the sand and water, following imaginary trails. "What is it, Sammy?" I ask, when he stops and paws anxiously at the sand. I squat and uncover half of a pink crab; Samson barks at it, sniffs it, then loses interest and pulls me onward.

The first time Naomi kissed me, I started laughing while her lips were still on mine; my laughter bubbled into her mouth, and her teeth clicked hard against mine. I pulled away, apologizing and still laughing, as nervous, I explained, as a teenager. She gripped my arms tightly, held my gaze, and said my name in a tone so full of urgency and promise that I shivered with anticipation. The love had come as quickly, and as smoothly, as the lovemaking.

I have forgotten how to plan meals only for myself, to consult no other opinions. I have started taking baths, and once, in the middle of shampooing, I have caught myself singing. There are days when I almost feel strong. And then there are times when I collapse like a crumbling house, sinking down onto my knees with terrible scraping sobs because the woman on television smiled in a way that reminded me. It was in one of those broken-down moments that I dialed Naomi's sister's apartment, conscious of no other source of solace than the sound of her voice. The phone was off its cradle, though, and the busy signal was like an accusation.

The breeze that comes off the water makes me wish I had grabbed a sweater on my way out of the house. Gray clouds are drifting in from offshore, and I wonder if May is too early in the season for a thunderstorm. Samson lifts his leg on the wet sand, and I tell him it is time to turn back; he looks up at me when I say his name, tongue lolling.

"Wanna jog it?" I ask the dog, and we run together back down the strip of beach. I am breathing hard by the time we reach home; I let Samson off his leash and pour myself a glass of water.

Upstairs, in the bedroom, I watch the dark clouds gather. Naomi used to love walking along the shoreline, then retreating up here with me and watching the sky darken. The bed is a warm nest. I lie down, pull the quilt over me, remembering...

I turn to her, raining soft kisses on her neck, tasting salt with the tip of my tongue. She leans her head back, closes her eyes as I begin to unbutton her shirt. I scrape my teeth along her collarbone, kiss my way down the open row of buttons.

It is the heat of Naomi's body that makes me moan, long and deep in my throat. She responds with a soft sigh, tugs at my shirt until we are curled against each other, my breasts against hers, bellies touching. The rhythm of her breathing, her heartbeat moves inside of me and awakens something in my stomach and cunt; a strong desire begins to stir and I whisper her name, feel her mouth under mine. Our thighs, still encased in jeans, tighten against each other. When the first raindrops begin to streak the windowpane, we are naked together on top of the blanket. I kiss her navel, the sharp jut of her hipbones, her soft fur. The lightning is a staccato illumination of our soft and moving bodies. Her hands clench and unclench on my shoulders, in my hair. She cries out as I trace the swell of her clitoris with my tongue, slide my arms under her thighs, bring her to my mouth again, and again, and again.

I wake just before dawn and open the window a few inches to let in the salty air. Last night's storm has stirred the usually placid sound so that small waves are washing upon the shore. Mornings like these, I think of returning to the small room next to the bedroom, the room that Naomi and I agreed would be my sculpting studio. I have not entered it since she left me. Sometimes, walking past its closed door, I press myself against the opposite wall, wanting to be as far away as possible from the possibility of entering. Sometimes I think about what I left in my studio the last time I was inside-weeks ago-and heat water for tea and open a book.

But last night I dreamt about wet clay, about what I had begun shaping, about what was waiting for me behind the door.

I have sculpted the figures of nearly everyone I have ever loved; and, many times over, I have sculpted the child I once was, the face I see in the mirror. I have even sculpted animals, small triangular faces and curved backs. I shape the figures I find waiting for me in the clay, deliver them, coax them out with the care and providence of a midwife. My best pieces hold a faint luminosity in their slow, full curves. In the clay beneath my fingers, the naked body finds an angelic resolution.

My inactivity has been like a long sleep. The lick of waves upon the shoreline reminds me of tiny hands and makes me long to work again. I stand outside the door of my studio for a long time and think about the silence that has coated me like ice for so long; I consider the fact that what insulates can be, at the same time, what keeps us numb.

I ache to begin again.

Weeks ago, before Naomi left, I had started with the head; it is a cold gray stare that meets me when I open the door. I walk closer, appreciating, through the turmoil in my belly, the quality of my rough work. I have gotten the shape of her head, neck, and shoulders exactly right. The nose is sloppy, though, and the mouth isn't there at all; and the eyes-well, the eyes are expressionless. I wet my hands at the sink in the corner and spread my knives and brushes on the table beside the mass of clay. I bring pitcher after pitcher from the sink until the statue is soft enough to yield to my touch; I lift my hands and seek the angles of her cheekbones in the clay. So many nights have I cradled her head close to me-so often have I mapped the terrain of her body with my fingertips-that my hands know just what is needed, and they work without hesitation.

I leave the face unfinished for now and shape the curve of the breasts, the slope of the shoulders, the arc of the biceps. I decide to sculpt her seated, reclining, one arm dangling by her side, the other resting on her stomach. Hours pass. When I become thirsty, I drink from the pitcher. Naomi's hands, so familiar, are easy to sculpt; I linger over them, until the wet, gray clay becomes an answer to her warm flesh.

My own hands are testimonies to my work-they are hard and unkempt. Naomi once clasped them in hers and asked me if I would sculpt her; but then it was I who quailed in the face of a love so strong I doubted my ability to tell it properly and wholly. Later that spring, the two of us sat on the empty beach and dug holes in the sand for the freezing water to find and fill; and I recognized the slow, constant motion of my love for her as the same flame that I bring to my best work.

There is a certain night that I think about sometimes, a couple of months before Naomi left. I woke up to darkness and the bed shaking: her shoulders were twitching, the muscles in her legs spasming. The sheets were wet with sweat. I grasped Naomi's shoulders, said her name loudly until she opened her eyes and stared, feverish and confused. I held her trembling body against me as she asked, hollowly, "Where am I?" The flu that blossomed in Naomi that night kept her in bed for almost a week afterward; but it was the vacancy in her eyes, the absence of warmth in her voice, that frightened me to the core. I learned, that night, what it was like to lose her.

I sculpt the delicate folds between her thighs as the last light of sunset is fading. I work by lamplight now. I knead the long muscles of her thighs and calves, and I press my thumbs into the arches of her feet. I minister to this replica of her body, turning aside to wet my hands, turning back to my craft, with a rhythm as steady as a cradle.

The best sculptors are gifted with a kind of sixth sense, a power of premonition that guides their hands to precisely the spot where the next touch is needed. Michelangelo had this gift, had known that the Muse is always about us; it is we who must be still enough in our hearts to hear her, to understand her direction and follow without protest. I sculpt my old lover and think about the gentle sabotage that only those who know us well can perform upon us; the clues she had offered me-out of pity, perhaps-went overlooked. Had I suspected the inconstancy of her love, for even a moment? I will never admit it; but my hands shaping the clay move with the rhythm of a farewell: good-bye, good-bye.

It is a piece like no other. The sculpture holds grace in every line and glistens with a smooth, living beauty. The angle of her hips, the hollow of her neck: I have captured all of it. Only the brows and mouth are incomplete; I pour a generous libation over the forehead, emptying the pitcher.

I called her on the phone to ask her to come back, to beg her if necessary; the emptiness she left when she went away paralyzed me with fear. The pattern of living without her was one I had happily forgotten, have had to learn again, slowly, as a survivor remembers how to walk, as a student begins the study of an old language. I smooth the statue's brow into a faraway look, full of the distance between a woman and her past; its lips I make as full and sensual as a kiss. Before I leave the statue to seal itself into dryness, before I carry myself out of the studio and through the living room and to my bed, I press my own mouth against the statue's for one moment-to imprint tiny lines onto the statue's lips: a proof of completion.

Silence on Fire

Joanna Lundy/Solomon

I get in trouble from Fowler for showing up late to class. She sends me to the office to get a late slip. I sit for a long time at my desk, just staring out the window.

"If you're not here to work, then maybe you shouldn't be here," says Fowler.

I want to shout, "Fuck off, you bitch!" but instead I say I'm not feeling well and ask if I can get some studio time later in the week.

Fowler's face softens for a moment. "I'm sorry," she says. "I didn't mean to bark at you. Go. Come back and see me when you want more time."

I make it into the washroom in time to barf again. This time, just water, but it winds me. Someone knocks on my cubicle.

"Are you okay?" I recognize Amy's voice.

"Go away." I puke some more.

"Do you want me to get help?"

"Just leave me alone."

"Open up the door or I'll crawl under."

"Suit yourself."

Amy crawls under. "God, you look awful."

"Thanks." I flush the toilet.

"What are you going to do?"

"Sit here until I stop throwing up."

Silence. Then Amy says, "You really freaked me out, you know."

"Look, if I freak you out so much then don't hang out with me."

Silence. "Look, I didn't stop caring about you."

"Is this some kind of half-assed apology? 'Cause you're full of shit. You don't leave people you care about."

Amy looks stunned, like I've hit her. I expect her to slap me in the face, but she just sits there.

"I thought if I left you, you'd go see the school counselor. I didn't think things would get worse. I'm sorry I left. You're right, it was a lame apology. Well, now that I've been an asshole, do you want to tell me what's going on?"

"Nope. I don't want to barf more. I'm trying not to think about it and every time I do, I just feel raw."

"Okay. How about we kiss and make up?"

"Just what did you have in mind? I've got vomit breath, you know."

"What's a little barf between friends?"

I lie back against the cold white toilet and laugh. "Stop. It hurts my stomach to laugh."

"I'm serious," says Amy.

"What, you want to kiss me right here, in the john?"

Amy nods. "I'm serious."

"What kind of kiss?"

"Chocolate."

My heart leaps to my throat. It's as if a wild bird took flight and got caught at the base of my tongue. I can't speak. Amy leans forward. I lean forward and shut my eyes. My nose hits hers. We laugh. Her mouth is soft and full and rich. Velvet and sweet. I feel dizzy and drunk.

"Chocolate, huh?"

"You haven't tasted the inside of this chocolate yet."

I pull away from Amy's arms.

"Don't play games with me. Don't make promises you can't keep. What about your boyfriend?"

"I don't know. I wasn't thinking about Mike right now."

"And what were you thinking of?"

"That kissing you was like kissing a guy, only better. I feel kinda stunned."

"Well, I'm not some experiment."

"Oh, God Sarah, I had no idea I felt this way about you. I've never kissed a girl before. I don't want to think about it, 'cause than I'll get scared to do it again. And I want to do it again."

This time Amy keeps her eyes open and manages to not bang my nose. She parts my mouth with her tongue, then runs her lips down my neck. It burns where she kisses me. I wind my fingers through her braids and pull her close.

"I feel so wild," Amy whispers into my hair. "Ahh girl, you are fine. Why did we wait so long?"

No, I didn't dream it all up. It really happened. Amy really kissed me. I feel joy burst through my blood, like a train speeding through darkness into dawn. I thought I had lost her and afterward Amy held me in the john as I cried. She rocked me, like a mother rocking a child to sleep.

That was two days ago and I've been kissing Amy whenever I can. It's kinda tricky at school, it's kinda like walking a tightrope and trying to not look down at the ground. We haven't been caught yet, but it's only a question of time before that happens—the risks we've been taking are too great. I haven't thought too much about my dad's death. It's on the other side of the fence with "before Amy kissed me." Mostly I don't have words to describe how I feel: it's as if the sun parted storm clouds and a soft rain is falling into the earth, only I'm the earth and I'm feeling fertile and creative and I have all of these ideas pouring out of me and I'm sketching them out so I can capture them before I lose them.

The days are getting shorter. I feel a chill on my skin as I sit by my bedroom window. There's a little bird hopping along the ledge, brown with a little red breast. I am not moving. My pencil is making soft, scratchy sounds across paper. The bird is very still. I hold out my hand, but I don't have any food and it flies away. I'm in this moment where the sun is hot across my face, the sky is a pale eggshell blue, and the wind has a chill. My arms are bumpy cold. I feel safe, like nothing bad can happen to me. I'm outside of time and death. I am in the middle of a strange peace. I don't want this peace to end. It's like I've come home to myself and Amy is part of this. I'm terrified of losing her, but in this moment I just feel safe. Amy is coming over tomorrow night. I want to hang on to this feeling of calm. I want it to go on and on. And I can already feel time flapping her wings at me.

I am lying in my bed. It has a runner of eyelet lace that falls under the sheets and touches the dust on the floor. The pillows have crocheted lace along the edge of their cases, yellowed from age. On my bed is my favorite quilt. It's been in my mother's family for a long time, made from scraps of colorful fabric. On the underside, I noticed a Jewish star motif; I had to look really hard to see it. It's hidden in there like everything in my mother's family.

Amy loves my bed. Last night we traced the Jewish star together. Amy got her period last night. I was rocking her cunt with my knee and felt her wiry hair and then this rush of something hot and wet on my leg. She moaned, and I thought, *Oh my god, she's coming.* I was so excited that I went down on her. I've never done it before. She moaned more and pulled my hair so tight I couldn't get my breath. When I licked her there was a sharp iron taste in my mouth and she was slippery. When I pulled out my hand I saw blood. I stared at my hand. Amy pulled my head up.

"What's the matter, babe?"

I was freaked out. "Did I cause you to bleed? God, I'm sorry."

Amy moaned with a laugh that shook her whole body. "Girl, you are too funny. It's my period."

I pulled away from her and wrapped the quilt tightly around me. "I thought I'd hurt you."

"Baby, let me in there. I didn't mean to laugh at you." She curled up against my back. I could feel her nipples harden against me. "Let me make you feel good." Her feet slid over my legs. "How did you know what to do? Have you ever been with a girl before? You'll have to help me. Tell me what you want."

I spoke slowly, my words coming from far away: "You're my first. I didn't know how to do it. It just felt natural. It just felt like the most natural thing in the world. And then I thought I'd hurt you. I can't bear the thought of you getting hurt, of losing you. Amy, I'm scared. What are we doing? How is this going to work?"

"Shh, I'm here." Amy buried her face in my neck. "Turn around so I can hold you. We don't have to make out. Let's make a tent and pretend that the rest of the fucked-up world of teachers and parents and adults are on the outside and we can do what ever we like in here."

And that's how we discovered the Jewish star on the inside of the quilt. And how in our tent, I got turned on and wanted her to go down on me. I couldn't find the words to ask. But she knew. Her tongue teased at my clit until it was swollen and hard. When I could not fight the swelling anymore, it burst and waves of pleasure flooded me. Amy held me when I came, looking into my eyes. I love you, her eyes said. She traced Amy loves Sarah between my breasts with her blood. And I traced Sarah loves Amy between hers. And we slept afterward like two wooden spoons, carved into the flesh of our bodies.

I feel like an eagle soaring on air. I feel home in my skin. This is who I am, this is whom I desire and it's not that fucked-up crap like, I'm going to marry a man and have his babies. I can't pretend who I am. What name do I give myself? Lesbian—too formal—lezzie—too rude. Queer—maybe. Gay—maybe. Dyke. I am a dyke. Dyke, hard K like fuck. Hard on the outside. Soft on the inside, where only Amy can see.

Amy is waking up. Making soft little snorting noises through her nose. Her skin is brown satin. There's a fine bead of sweat above her upper lip.

She opens her eyes, smiles. And says, "Are you writing about me? Come here."

Amy's gone home. We had our first fight yesterday morning in the shower. Amy thinks we should go to the Gay & Lesbian Center or the Vancouver Lesbian Connection—the VLC—and find out how to have safer sex. We had an argument about it because she wanted me to go alone. She's scared of someone from the synagogue seeing her go into the VLC. I said that was bullshit, that it wasn't fair to place the whole thing on me. She got freaked out about the blood thing. I know it wasn't really safe, but all they teach us in school is condoms condoms condoms. Straight sex and condoms and don't share needles. So we had our first fight—in the shower. Aunt Lucy raised her eyebrows when we came out half an hour later from a steamy bathroom, but she didn't say a word to us.

I'm going to phone the VLC and find out what hours they're open, and Amy is coming with me. After the shower, we lay on my bed with our wet towels wrapped around us. Talked some more, holding hands. I love to touch the soft skin on the underside of her hands. I get this rush just holding her hand.

Amy says, "I want you to see that counselor at school." I hold my breath. She raises my hand up to her mouth and kisses it softly. "I'm worried about you," she says.

"Do you think something's wrong with me?"

"Something's really hurting you inside, baby."

"I can figure it out myself. I've got my art. I've got you."

"What if I let you down when you really need me, or you can't reach me by phone? What then, who would you go to?"

I am silent.

"Look, last year I took a peer counseling group. It was pretty cool. We did a one-day workshop on suicide prevention. It was about building a safety net and telling as many people as possible."

I pull my hand away from hers. "I'm not suicidal."

She turns my wrists over. "Then why did you hurt yourself?"

We both stare at the horizontal scars across my wrists.

"Babe, someone besides me is going to notice soon. What about your mother, hasn't she noticed?"

"My mother's not around to notice. Look, I'm not trying to seriously hurt myself, I have other things to do to numb out the pain, and when they don't work, I do this."

"What pain?"

"I can't talk about it with you. I can't. Don't make me. I don't want to see a counselor. 'Cause I want to see myself through my own eyes. Like what happens if she talks me out of what I feel? Or doesn't get it? Or what if she lets me down right when I need her? Maybe she won't believe me."

"Why wouldn't she believe you?"

"Sometimes I don't believe myself, you know. It seems so fantastic, like I made it up or something. But I know it really happened. If I tell a counselor, maybe she'll think I made it up. What's wrong with my art? It's not gonna fail me. It's kept me alive so far."

Amy is silent. I can see a tiny bead of sweat above her upper lip. I want to kiss it away, swallow the salt from her body to cleanse the pain from mine. I want her to hold me. This is what I want more than anything now. I can feel the heat between our bodies, and I am crying. Amy pulls me to her. My skin is thirsty for her touch, the warmth of her skin against mine. Her mouth is on my nipple, licking and sucking, pulling and biting. Her tears run down my breasts, onto my arm. I slide onto her, take her face between my hands and kiss the salt away. I hear myself promise that I will see a counselor.

I don't make promises easily. It had something to do with the salt of Amy's tears on my arm and knowing she loves me. Love makes you do crazy things, I guess. This promise is one that I have to keep, but I don't feel good about it. I feel a chill over my arms, a goose-bumpy feeling. I think I'm giving away a part of myself for Amy. I don't believe in counselors. They have this power, even if they don't own it. That's why my art is so important. I don't want a counselor to cure me, so I can't paint. All of the stuff that tortures me comes up in my art. I live for my art. I'd die without it. Why did I make this promise to Amy? Going to a counselor isn't the only way to heal yourself. I wish I had been strong enough to say no to Amy. I was afraid I'd lose her if I didn't promise.

Amy and I are having lots of sex.

She slept over on Saturday night. We spent the whole night touching and kissing. We wandered to the local women's sex toy store, late Saturday afternoon, after Amy went to Or Shalom with her parents. We giggled over the leather harnesses and dildoes. I don't want to wear a penis to fuck Amy. I'm a girl, not a boy. Amy's interested, not me. But we did agree to buy some latex and gloves. They had a bin full of them.

Having safer sex is new. We're going to get checked for STD's next week. Amy's found this cool doctor who's bisexual. We're planning to go next Monday after school. Until we know we're clean, we're using gloves and latex when we go down on each other. The brochures don't explain lots, just the basics. Amy and I have a lot of laughs experimenting on each other.

"God, I hate the latex," says Amy. "How long do we have before Aunt Lucy gets home?"

"Another hour. Please don't suck my clit with rubber. What do you think of getting your clit pierced?"

"Nah, what if you couldn't get off?"

"True, it's the only drug that's legal. Amy?"

"Yeah, girl."

"Do you ever think we're doing anything wrong? Do you ever wonder what people would say if they knew?"

"What's worrying you, babe?"

"I just wish we could hold hands in public. And I wish it were safe to be out in school. I wish this wasn't a big secret. I wish you could tell Mike and not be afraid of what he'd do. Keeping it a secret makes me feel like we're doing something wrong."

Amy is silent for a long time.

"Let's make out and pretend it will all go away," she says.

Her breath is hot against my leg, where she is curled up to me. Her kisses reach my hair, which is moist. I'm throbbing inside and I want to say, *But it doesn't go away, Amy.*

Her fingers reach inside me. My silence is on fire. There

are millions of birds with fire-tipped wings and they fly low over water, until the flames of their wings are extinguished without a sound.

Ofra and Tal
Caril Behr

Tal was my lover for three years, and every day during that time she and her mother Ofra phoned each other to scream and fight. It wasn't twenty-minute skirmishes or half-hour disagreements they embarked upon, but operatic productions on a grand scale lasting for hours and days. Both of them frequently slammed the phone down and then redialed to offer more hysterical versions of recently screeched arias. I could never figure out exactly what they were fighting about. I doubt that they knew themselves. They could not let go of each other, and fighting was a way of hanging on.

Ofra insisted that she couldn't be deprived of telephonic contact with Tal, so she paid for us to have a phone installed. She also paid our phone bill; otherwise Tal and I might not have lasted the distance.

When she's not screaming, Ofra has an impeccable eye for the universally lovely. She is a graceful woman with a razor-sharp instinct for popular tastes. She might look like a folksy eccentric in hand-woven fabrics, but when it comes to selling things, she's got a magic touch. Her London gallery is not the least bit intimidating in spite of the exclusive surroundings. She knows how to make people feel at home. They flock to her and spend money.

During the time that Tal lived with me, their marathon howlings left her frazzled and exhausted. At first, I was quietly solicitous. I held and comforted her. I racked my brain for words of intelligent advice, but nothing helped. Later I became indignant and tried in vain to limit their repetitive dramas. It got to the point where my nerves couldn't take another second of it and I very nearly left Tal, but then I became amused and indifferent. I let them get on with tormenting each other and got on with my own work through the noise.

One day when I came home in the late afternoon, I could hear Tal screaming before I even got indoors. She slammed the phone down and quivered with rage, waiting for it to ring again. When it did, she pounced on it and yelled, "I hate you, drop dead!" Then she disconnected the phone, burst into tears, and threw herself at me, expecting to be comforted.

"How do you know that was Ofra phoning back? It could have been someone for me!" I stood, arms hanging limply at my sides, while she buried her face in my neck, crying snotty tears. I had never before seen her do anything so assertive as pulling out the phone plug—otherwise, I would have shown a good deal more impatience.

It was all because Ofra had phoned to tell Tal that she was a lesbian. She had been denying it all her life. Now, on the eve of her sixtieth birthday, Ofra thought it was about time to come out. Time was running out on her, she said, and she wanted to be herself before it became too late. She simply could not go on repressing her true self a minute longer. The moment of truth had arrived.

"Surely this calls for celebration, not lament!" I was taken aback by Tal's weeping.

"You don't understand" Tal said. "She's doing this to spite me. This has got nothing to do with being true to herself at all. It's just another lunatic ploy to take my life away from me."

"Stop being so bloody melodramatic and self-centered. Your mother does have a life apart from you, believe it or not."

"That's where you're wrong. Ofra doesn't have an independent bone in her body, nor does she have an original thought in her brain. Whatever I've done, she's copied. Whatever I've achieved, she's tried to undermine or belittle. When I was growing up, I had to fight her tooth and nail for the right to have a personality of my own. She used to criticize me until I became a gibbering wreck. Then, when I stood up for myself and made a change, no matter how small, she'd copy me and say it was her idea all along. I wish you'd see that she's trying to absorb and consume me. My life is a daily battle to exist."

"Ofra can't engage in this struggle on her own. Why don't you let go for one second and try to see that Ofra's concerns can be like yours, without actually being yours. If she wasn't your mother, you'd think her coming out was really cool."

"If Ofra's going to be a lesbian, then I can't be a lesbian!"

That remark got up my nose.

"If this is a competition, then you might as well change your gender, or even your species. Come out as a fish." I didn't mean to be inflammatory, but it was the end of a long workday and I was tired.

"Why are you winding me up? Can't you see how upset I am?"

"You've got it so cushy it's unbelievable. You've no idea what it's like to stand up to homophobic shit from your mother, and I mean of the poisonous variety, where she says she would rather see you dead than gay."

The argument died down for an hour or two, but later in the evening Tal said, "Maybe I'm bisexual."

"Maybe, but why compromise? You could find yourself a bearded patriarch. Come out wearing a hideous head scarf. Give Ofra a house full of grandchildren. That should keep you both screaming for the rest of your natural lives."

"Bitch!"

Tal came flying, but I was ready for her. I caught her arms and wrestled her to the ground, where I held her in a restraining lock. Tal is a delicate little person and it was easy enough for me to overpower her, but that didn't stop her from biting and spitting at me.

When she had calmed down, I started undressing her. She did not resist, nor did she respond. I found myself regarding the removal of each garment with grim triumph. I squeezed her nipples through the fabric of her bra and felt them harden against my fingertips. The more she gasped, the harder I squeezed. I tugged at a silky tuft of armpit hair and nipped her shoulder. The softness of her skin almost made me weep, but I hardened my heart. After I'd pulled off her jeans, I drove my thumb into the hollow of her navel. Her eyelids flickered and her lips parted. I used my knuckles to make rapid twisting movements against her cunt through her panties, until they became wet.

"Look at me," I ordered her. "Why won't you look at me?" She turned her head away from me, but I'd rather she had slapped me in the face. That would at least have been an acknowledgment. I penetrated her roughly with two fingers and thumbed her clitoris. She came. It was over quickly, a mere knee-jerk reaction. I could tell. Her body was with me on the floor, but her self had floated off somewhere out of reach. It was horrible. It was painful. I did not remove my own clothes, and she made no attempt to reach out and touch me. The tougher I acted, the more desperate and vulnerable I felt. I wanted Tal to do something, anything, to reassure me, but she didn't.

The daily phone calls continued, but they changed in tone. Tal became less childish, more clipped and sarcastic. Clearly, some change was brewing inside her. She resigned from her job as a photographic archivist, announcing that she wanted to visit her father in Israel. After that, she wanted to travel for six months on her own. My heart sank at the thought of letting her go, but I could see the sense of it. Tal had lived with Ofra until she was twenty-eight. No sooner had she come out, than she'd met me and fallen straight into my arms. She moved in with me on the proverbial second date. In all her life, she had never spent a day away from either Ofra or me.

On the day of her departure, Ofra drove us to Heathrow, where the three of us kissed and hugged and wept and clung to one another. We blocked the entrance to passport control, causing other travelers to issue irritable rebukes. Eventually, Tal peeled herself away and was swallowed up in the crowd. After that, Ofra came back to my flat and we mooned about like a couple of lost souls. I felt as if a major organ had been removed. She was almost ill with anxiety at the thought of Tal being so far away.

The days and weeks passed and I saw a lot of Ofra, who was generous to a fault. She cooked me sumptuous meals and treated me to the ballet and opera, buying tickets I could never afford. In return I took her out on the scene and introduced her to women, so that she could make connections of her own. She phoned me every day and we had long rambling conversations, during which we exchanged confidences and analyzed the world and its ills. Tal wrote to both of us and phoned us both. She was a magnet, drawing us together and pulling us toward her. I wrote Tal three, sometimes four, letters a week, and Ofra wrote to her every day.

One day Tal phoned and said in a breathless voice, "Darling I've got fabulous news. I hope you'll be happy for me."

I felt instantly sick and knew exactly what was coming. She went on to say that she'd met a man, someone much older than herself, very refined, gentle, liberated and cultured. He treated her like a princess. He doted on her. He was a math professor at Haifa University and had a charming villa in the Galilee on the shore of Lake Kinneret. He had asked Tal to marry him and she had accepted his offer.

"Please don't be angry," she said.

"Why the fuck not? I've got every right to be angry."

"But you can't, I need your blessing…"

These were the very words I'd been dreading since the moment of her departure. I'd tried to strengthen and defend myself against this inevitability by anticipating it, but when it came, I just fell apart. I said the first words that came into my head.

"A plague on both your heads," I screamed and sobbed. "May you take ill and waste away. I hope some maniac blows you up on the way to the wedding." Then I slammed the phone down and pulled out the plug.

My friends rallied round me as soon as they heard the news, and they condemned Tal in no uncertain terms.

"You're better off without her," they said. "She's so spoiled and childish. She was a drain on your energy. You'll meet someone else."

"Yes, yes," I agreed. I conjured up in detail all Tal's annoying habits, like flossing her teeth and leaving the grunged-up bits of dental floss lying on the bed. I thought about how she used to let a little pile of Tampax applicators accumulate next to the bath, and how she would wriggle and flail in her sleep, dragging the duvet off me onto her side of the bed. This made me realize how desperately I wanted her. I simply cried and cried. Ofra was most indignant on my behalf.

"I don't know how Tal could do this to you. She's no daughter of mine. I'm ashamed of her. I'll never speak to her again."

"Yes, Ofra, we'll see." How many times in the past had I heard Tal and Ofra say those words? It was an empty refrain.

One Friday night Ofra invited me over for a meal and I went. She had gone to great trouble, preparing all my favorite dishes and setting the table for a romantic candlelit dinner. There was even a tastefully wrapped present waiting for me. When I opened it I found a turquoise silk bandanna, which she showed me how to tie with a neat flat knot, letting her long, cool fingers linger on my neck. It wasn't until after we'd eaten, when we were lounging on her comfortable sofa cradling brandy glasses, that I realized she was coming on to me. She'd been prowling around me nervously, finding excuses to touch me all evening. Then she asked out of the blue:

"Are you butch or femme?"

"Figure it out, Ofra! Why don't you go down on me? Let's see if you can make me come," I teased.

She did precisely that, with such skill and confidence that she took my breath away. Then she let me reciprocate, and pretty soon we were in her bed, devouring each other with unbridled passion. I spent the night with her, and the next morning she brought me breakfast in bed. We made love in the shower and on the carpet, where I lay back and let her smother me with kisses. It was a relief to let her engulf and consume me.

"I suppose we'd better tell Tal," she said presently.

"Oh yes, we must!" I felt savage glee and wanted to create as much emotional havoc as possible. "I think you should be the one to tell her, but don't phone her now, wait until I've gone."

Later in the day when I got home, the phone rang, as I knew it would.

"How dare you do this to me? I feel so betrayed."

"Dear, dear, maybe you should have some therapy, or perhaps your math professor can comfort you with an equation or two." She slammed the phone down.

Now that Ofra and I were lovers, I basked in the attention and affection she bestowed. She showered me with thoughtful little surprises and seemed to anticipate my needs. I absorbed her like a sponge. She wanted me to move in with her, but I needed to keep my own space, so I stayed in my flat, which is conveniently near my work, and I spent all my weekends with Ofra. On weeknights she would phone me and we would talk for hours. We never found anything to fight about, and I think Ofra felt appreciated at last.

Our affair started in the early spring. We were halfway through July, when Ofra said one day, "I got a phone call from my sister in Israel. She's going to visit her son in California for three weeks and her flat will be empty. She wants me to stay there, feed the cat, and look after her plants while she's away. Come with me. I'll pay your fare. You'll love it out there. Her flat is in Netanya, right on the beach. It's a perfect place for a holiday."

I agreed to go. It did indeed sound like a perfect place for a holiday, and I felt ready for a confrontation with Tal. I knew that Ofra was desperate to see her. Tal, it seemed, had given up on her plans for independent travel. She had moved into the math professor's lakeside villa, rehearsing for a life of kept woman-hood. She went to yoga and pottery classes. They planned to marry in the autumn, early in the Jewish new year, after Yom Kippur. I could imagine Tal in a white wedding gown, with her jet-black curls and smoldering eyes, a single string of river pearls about her neck. The thought made me want to smash something, preferably Tal's head.

So off we went on our seaside holiday. I quickly acclimatized to ninety degrees of heat and spent my days splashing about in the ocean or lying naked on the secluded balcony of the flat, soaking up the sun as it poured in from above. Then came the day of confrontation. Ofra and I waited for Tal's arrival in agitated silence.

As soon as Tal walked through the door, the two of them burst into tears and fell into each other's arms. They kissed and caressed and clung together with a desperation I had never seen before and haven't seen since. They keened and wailed. They stroked and licked each other. They did not see me leave the flat.

As I walked down the road to the beach, I knew they were already lovers, and that from that moment on, nothing but death could tear them apart. I ached all over with resignation and the recognition that this was what they had both been longing for all of this time. This was what they had been fighting and trying to avoid. I felt no anger. All my anger was spent. I grieved for what was never mine in the first place.

When I got back to the flat after several hours of wandering aimlessly, it reeked of their lovemaking. They were red-eyed, exhausted, and naked. Tal cradled Ofra on her lap, as their clothes lay scattered over every surface. When they saw me, they reached out and drew me sobbing into their embrace. Together they undressed me, all three of us crying and laughing and clinging together as if this were the last day on earth for all time. It felt as if it was.

Emboldened by her time away from me, Tal maneuvered me into a position of helplessness, where I lay contained within Ofra's arms. Tal took my face in both her hands, looking steadily into my eyes.

"You belong to me," she said. "You always have. You always will." She kissed me. She did more than kiss me. She sucked the breath out of me. She licked the roof of my mouth, her tongue aflame. With excruciating tenderness they traced the contours of my body. I saw their hands cross over my breasts. Their fingers touched. I registered the shock wave at the very center of my being. I arched my back, offering my cunt up to their enjoined hands. Now I had become the magnet and they both belonged to me. The more I opened up to their searching fingers, the hungrier I became. My desperation fueled their enjoined desire, carrying us from one orgasm to another. Our limbs ached. Our throats became parched from crying out, but there was no stopping us.

That night and every subsequent night of our stay in Israel we slept together in a tangle on the bed. Actually, not a lot of sleeping took place. We could not leave one another alone, and we carried on until we were senseless. We made spectacles of ourselves in restaurants, eating off one another's plates, feeding one another and transferring food from mouth to mouth. We kissed passionately and fondled one another intimately in theaters, art galleries, supermarkets, anywhere. The sight of ordinary people going about their daily business drove us to frenzies of erotic display. Our public exhibitions fueled our private devourings. We were simply possessed.

We had planned a pilgrimage to Jerusalem, where we intended to intone a blessing at the wailing wall, but we never got there. We never got there because we couldn't get out of bed. It required no more than a look or a touch to get us going. A finger would gently caress the soft skin on the inside of an elbow, and the wave of pleasure would surge through all three of our bodies in a huge swell.

One evening after dark we ran naked into the warm ocean. Like nymphs in the night we danced on the deserted beach and sang a song of self-blessing. On the way home we stuffed our underwear into a crack in a passing wall, beside ourselves with mirth. We needed no witnesses. We had invented ourselves and belonged to one another.

As for Tal's math professor, she abandoned him without a flicker of emotion or regret. She coolly broke off her engagement on the phone and wouldn't even go back to collect her things. She dispatched Ofra to return the ring and fetch her belongings. The wretched man was in a state of shock. He had no idea what was behind this sudden rejection. As neither Ofra nor Tal would enlighten him, he was left to draw his own conclusions.

Eventually, the holiday came to an end and we had to return to London. Both Ofra and Tal begged me to move in with them.

"I'll have a bed made specially for three," Ofra said, but I declined.

I would not lay claim to anything as elevated as rational thought, but I knew a chapter was closing and we had to let it go.

I have had lovers since, but my relationships with other women fizzle out almost before they've begun. I have not found anyone who fires my imagination or kindles my desire the way they do. I see and speak to them all the time, both on the phone and in the flesh. Not a day goes by when we don't have contact of some kind. Tal works with Ofra in the gallery now. They never let each other out of sight, except to go to the toilet; even then, I have my doubts.

Inevitably, I am their lover, and when I visit them, I share their bed. My body is so deeply responsive to their touch that I can make myself come just thinking about them. Occasionally, I feel the need to assert my sense of separate personhood with a gesture, such as driving home at four in the morning, but more and more I can't be bothered. Who am I kidding, anyway?

Since my own parents have disowned me, Ofra and Tal are all I have in the world. If anything bad were to happen, I know they would never abandon me. But it goes much deeper than that. My speech is peppered with their phrases. Their voices ring constantly in my head. I can feel when I'm thinking their thoughts, and I know when they are tuning into mine. My body aches if either of them is ill, and if I as much as sneeze, they materialize on my doorstep to shriek and fight over me. Whoever takes me on takes them on as well, for better or for worse.

A Blessing and a Curse

Karen Taylor

Ever since she'd come out into the leather scene, Deborah had watched the dykes around her incorporate ritual into their S/M play. The leather conferences she attended sometimes had workshops titled "S/M and Spirituality," or "S/M Ritual." She used to go to these workshops, but she found they left her flat. They did not speak to her. She was a Jew, she was a lesbian. These things were born in her. They were intertwined, without any internal struggle. She felt no disgust about or need to rebel against her childhood, filled with Hebrew classes and Young Judea, unlike many of her friends who tried to rebel against their Christian upbringing. Unfortunately, they never seemed to completely divorce themselves from Christian culture, even when practicing other religious rituals.

"Come on, Deborah, we're all going to do a full-moon ritual. You have to join us."

At first, she was amused and kindly turned them down, but soon she found their reactions were as uncompromising as those of any fundamentalist proselytizer: everyone must participate or be cast out, exiled. Deborah was all too familiar with oppression by the majority and the demand to conform to someone else's belief system. Her family had dealt with it for centuries, beginning with the Inquisition. Deborah's ancestors had moved from Spain to Morocco and Turkey and later to Cuba, eventually traveling north to the United States, all to escape such religious oppression. Five hundred years after her family left their home rather than become *conversos*, Deborah had no intention of going against family tradition. And so she stood aside when able, or did not attend events in which all were expected to participate in pagan rituals.

But a part of her craved her own ritual, one that drew from her own background, something to demonstrate to herself that her S/M and her Judaism could be celebrated together. She had expressed this desire to Rebecca. Rebecca, who was Reform, admitted that she didn't feel the need as strongly, but she was supportive. If it involved her dominating or hurting Deborah, she was in favor of it.

Rebecca. Deborah shivered when she thought of Rebecca, her stern Prussian features and ice-blue eyes, the cruel smile flickering on her lips. Rebecca was Deborah's lover, and her mistress. They had been together for nearly five years, although they had only recently moved in together, sharing a home. A room for Rebecca, a room for Deborah, a guest room—and a full dungeon in the basement. It was here that Deborah spent her most glorious moments. Rebecca's poise and controlled passion provided a vicious counterpoint to Deborah's emotionally charged pleas for mercy, which often burst into waves of orgasm as Rebecca pushed her harder and harder. When Rebecca praised her, holding her trembling body, Deborah knew that their relationship was all that she could ever desire.

It was the commitment ceremony of their friends Shani and Rabbit that was Deborah's catalyst. Unlike many of the women in the S/M community, whose New-Age spirituality often seemed an excuse for unusual technique, Shani and Rabbit were both deeply spiritual pagans. Shani, who taught at the university, was a specialist in the lesser-known Bantu tribes, and she had traced her own ancestry back nearly four hundred years to a fierce tribe that was finally wiped out by the Gandas. Rabbit reflected her nickname: she was a slight, small woman with nervous habits whose pale skin shown against Shani's majestic blackness. Deborah loved watching the two of them play, especially when Shani tied Rabbit's body in contorted positions, then tortured her labia, using the rings Shani had put in herself, finally rubbing Rabbit's clit to orgasm, while the small woman howled in pain and ecstasy. When Deborah received the invitation to their bonding ceremony, she was deeply honored and intrigued.

The ceremony took place out of doors, in a grassy meadow on private land owned by a friend. The area was lit by torches thrust into the ground around a clearing. As Deborah and Rebecca settled themselves on the grass with the other guests, four masked women holding skin drums and calabashes stepped out of the darkness and began a slow, throbbing beat. Following them were two figures. One Deborah identified immediately as Rabbit, crouched and naked, her slight body shivering and vulnerable. The second figure Deborah knew must be Shani—but what a figure she presented. Nude except for an animal-skin mask concealing her face, Shani was indeed a warrior. Shani stalked Rabbit, her height and powerful muscles accentuated by the lines and circles painted in clay across her arms, breasts, legs, slowly circling Rabbit until the smaller woman sat huddled, her liquid eyes staring up at the powerful figure above her. The drumming grew in intensity.

Shani opened her right hand, exposing a piece of black obsidian, one edge honed to razor sharpness. She again moved around Rabbit, her movements in beat with the drumming. Finally she stopped before her lover and pulled the mask away. The drumming grew faster as Shani opened her other hand and drew the obsidian point across her palm. As the blood poured out, the drummers stopped.

"My blood hunts for this one," she intoned, dropping to her knees. She rubbed her hand across Rabbit's neck, then down her body and between her legs. "This is my prey." The drumming began again, and Shani swayed hypnotically, her hand tracing bloody lines across Rabbit, as if she were gutting her lover. When she finished, Rabbit slowly pulled herself up to her knees. Her shivering had stopped, and her gesture to the drummers was strong and sure. The drumming stopped once again.

Taking the obsidian blade from Shani's hand, Rabbit said in a small but clear voice, "We are bound forever this way, the hunter and the prey." In one clean stroke, she drew the blade across her neck where the collarbone joined it, and she presented the wound to Shani, straining her body up and forward. With a cry Shani's mouth opened, and her teeth sank into Rabbit's neck, into the blood, as Rabbit screamed. The drumming began again, wildly beating as the two women's bodies, locked together, rolled across the clearing, their bodies shaking in ecstasy. With a shout, the watchers howled, leaping to their feet, clapping and stamping. Deborah joined in the mad dance as the circle of people moved to keep Shani and Rabbit in their center. She twirled and shouted, dancing to the drummers, to the music that sank into her bones and awakened her loins. Blood lust, thought Deborah, as Rabbit's shrieks pierced through the rumble of the crowd. This is what blood lust feels like.

The ritual and the image continued to fire Deborah's imagination when she and Rebecca returned home. Could it be possible to create a ritual as clearly expressive of her relationship with Rebecca? Something as obvious as the mezuzah on their front door, and as personal as the sweat of their shared release?

"Why not?" answered Rebecca. "Jews have a blessing for everything—there's probably a ritual somewhere for two women that somebody tried oh, a millennium or so ago. Didn't Ruth and Naomi have some sort of lesbian relationship?"

"That's a possible interpretation, but the intent of the story is something different," Deborah said. "You see, Ruth was Naomi's daughter-in-law. And—"

"Save the lecture for Shabbat, rabbi," Rebecca interrupted, yawning. "It's getting late. Why don't you work on it tomorrow? I wanna think about Rabbit's face when Shani bit into her neck—boy, that was hot!" She nuzzled Deborah's neck, nibbling and biting until they both forgot how late it was.

The next day, however, Deborah decided to begin her research. She started with a review of the women in the Torah.

No use copying a story of the men, although she flirted with the idea of the binding of Isaac as a demonstration of commitment. Was there anything in the women's accomplishments that did not have to do with marrying a famous man or having a famous baby? Her namesake, of course, was a judge and warrior, but the stories didn't suggest a ritual to her. As for the story of Esther, Deborah's feminism always revolted at the idea of a savior of Jews being basically the winner of a beauty contest. Where to go? There were five thousand years of text to choose from, covering everything from how many witnesses were required at a murder trial to how many hours to wait between eating meat and eating ice cream. She groaned, her head already beginning to ache from the immensity of the task she'd set for herself.

With a sigh, Deborah reopened her Torah. What was the week's *parsha*, anyway? *Mishpatim*, she noted, glancing at her calendar. The beginning of the list of civil laws the Ruler of the Universe gave immediately after the more familiar Ten Commandments. *Mishpatim* begins with the rights of persons, containing the so-often misunderstood "eye for an eye" passage that Christians were so apt to misinterpret as bloodthirstiness. It's as good a place to start as any, she thought, and she began to read.

EXODUS XXI *(mishpatim)*

"Now these are the ordinances which thou shalt set before them. If thou buy a Hebrew servant, six years he shall serve; and in the seventh he shall go out free for nothing."

Ah, yes, Deborah recalled. Jews could only keep other Jews as slaves for a set period of time before they were required to set them free. Her eyes quickly scanned the text, moving on to the laws about punishing murder...but wait. Something tickled her memory. Deborah returned to the beginning of the parsha and began reading more closely.

"But if the servant shall plainly say: I love my master, my wife, and my children; I will not go out free; then his master shall bring him unto God, and shall bring him to the door, or unto the door-post; and his master shall bore his ear through with an awl; and he shall serve him for ever."

Intriguing, thought Deborah. Scanning the commentary, she saw that the servant's declaration was required to be made publicly, to prevent the master from boring his servant's ear by force.

"It could work," she said to Rebecca, after reading her the parsha that evening. "And the text repeats itself in Deuteronomy, which won't be until summer—that gives us time to plan."

"I like it," Rebecca responded. "I'd been thinking about piercing you, anyway." Deborah lowered her eyes from her lover's face, feeling a flush rise from her chest and move its way upward. That night her dreams were filled with images of needles driving themselves into her ears, her nipples, her labia, and she came hard when Rebecca caned her the next morning.

Over the next several weeks Deborah searched the Mishnah, the oral text that gave greater outline to the commandments of the Torah. It was here that she learned that a slave who chose to remain in bondage was treated with a different level of respect. Should the slave have children while under this longer contract, the children were born free, and the master was expected to pay for their education and other needs.

"A relationship with benefits on both sides, while acknowledging who's the boss—yeah, it works," said Rebecca, when Deborah was reporting on her research.

"The book may be old, but it doesn't mean it's out of date," Deborah joked. "That's why we Jews endure."

"Yeah, well, you'll be enduring something tonight, in reward for your research," Rebecca warned her. "Get down in the dungeon, and wait for me." Deborah hurried downstairs, so as to be kneeling and naked by the time Rebecca joined her. This time Rebecca didn't tie her down but forced her to remain still, while she opened a box of hypodermic needles. "It's time to start practicing, my sweet slave," Rebecca said as she pinched a piece of Deborah's fleshy breasts between her fingers. As Deborah watched, Rebecca pushed the green-capped needle through the skin. As the needle invaded her body, Deborah gasped, yelping as it poked its way through the other side. A wave of dizziness washed over her. "Oh, yes," Rebecca whispered, picking up another needle, then a third. At the sixth needle pressing into and through her breast's flesh, Deborah felt herself beginning to float away. The sharp, pinpricking sensations tickled at her consciousness, pulling at her slightly as she drifted in a state of ecstasy. She dreamed of being a lifelong slave, each needle in her flesh marking another seven years of service to her mistress. She was hardly aware of Rebecca pulling the needles back out of her body, of returning upstairs to her bed; the line between consciousness and unconsciousness had been pierced by the needles and the memory her flesh held for them.

At Pesach, Deborah and Rebecca attended Lev's second seder, and, as usual, the conversation turned political—this time about the importance of gender on a *Bet Din*. Deborah was arguing for the importance of tradition in their planned ritual, but Rebecca's Reform liberalism was balking at the inherent sexism of the passage of commentary that insisted that the rabbinical court would have to be formed of three learned men, rather than three learned people. Benjamin, a teacher at the local Hebrew day school, agreed with Deborah's argument, while Tovah was firmly on Rebecca's side. Finally, Lev intervened.

"You, my little one, so serious in the face, you want tradition?" Lev said, smiling at Deborah. "So, *nu*, what is traditional about your household, other than you keep it kosher? Two women, sharing a bed? This balebosteh beating you and you thanking her for it?" Deborah blushed at Lev's frankness. He chuckled and put his hand over hers.

"Ah, *maidelah*, my suggestion is that you choose your guests carefully—I think you will find that you will have learned men and women there, and how you define your *Bet Din* will be up to you."

"You are at the top of our guest list, a genuine wise man," Rebecca exclaimed, giving Lev a hug. "And, of course, you two," she added, giving Benjamin a kiss on the cheek while she squeezed Tovah's thigh. "You heterosexual types will give the evening a sense of respectability."

"I'll give you respectability," grinned Tovah, squeezing

Rebecca back. "She'll give you even more, if you ask her," Benjamin added, as the group fell into laughter.

After the seder, Rebecca and Deborah continued to discuss their guest list.

"Shani and Rabbit, definitely, for their inspiration," decided Rebecca. "And I think Miriam and Greta, they've always been so helpful to me. That's five wise women and two wise men." But Deborah was still worried about gathering a traditional *Bet Din*, until one day the problem solved itself: Rebecca came home from work and reported that David was dating Saul.

"Can you believe they met at an Arab-Israeli forum?" Rebecca laughed. "It wasn't until they got back to Saul's apartment that they realized they had done each other in the baths only the week before!" Then Rebecca and Deborah looked at each other. "That's it!" Rebecca exclaimed.

"David and Saul, they'd be perfect," Deborah agreed. "With Lev and Benjamin, that gives me a great Bet Din plus an extra. But no more," she added. "That's a lot of cooking already! Thank *Ha-Shem* they all eat meat."

Rebecca kissed her. "True. But I have hard work to do, too— after all, I'm preparing your questioners."

Deborah shivered when she caught the glint in Rebecca's eye. That night they made love passionately, Rebecca twisting Deborah's nipples hard, triggering an orgasm from the sounds of Rebecca's screams.

Their evenings were busy through early summer. Deborah was pouring over her cookbooks with the same avid attention she had paid to the Mishnah only weeks earlier, planning out an elaborate menu. Rebecca would stay out late, visiting with

Miriam and Greta, or at Lev's house, returning home to question Deborah about ritual details, or to beat her savagely until Deborah begged for mercy.

"It's to get you in practice, my dearest," Rebecca would answer to Deborah's pleas.

Finally, the evening arrived, and so did their guests. Deborah was hurrying back and forth between the door and the kitchen, checking on dinner. Rabbit joined her in the kitchen as soon as she and Shani arrived, as did Tovah, a few minutes later, bringing a bottle of wine, and Saul, bearing a chocolate torte. Rebecca was in the living room, smiling and relaxed as she introduced Shani to David, complimenting Miriam on her new dress and congratulating Greta on her promotion, greeting Benjamin with *"Shabbat shalom,"* and giving Lev a kiss and a *"Gut Shabbos."* The house smelled of roasting chicken and fresh bread. Deborah had taken great care with the table, using her grandmother's linen tablecloth and covering the challah loaves with lovely embroidered covers her mother had made for her. She had decided to use Rebecca's silver wine cup, a gift from her bat mitzvah so many years ago, and it was placed next to the heavy crystal candlestick, the two white tapers already in place.

Finally, they gathered at the table, Lev and Benjamin in their yarmulkes, Tovah and Deborah wearing kerchiefs.

"Baruch ata adonai elohainu melech ha-olam, asher kidshanu b'mitsvotav, vitsivanu, lehadlik ner shel shabbat." Greta's clear voice led them as Miriam, Deborah, and Tovah shaded their eyes while the candles were lit. Then Lev's baritone boomed out the *kiddush.*

"Baruch ata adonai . . . boray p'ri ha-gafen." Lev drained the cup of wine, and the corners of his eyes crinkled in pleasure. The magic of Shabbat began to descend upon the gathering. Deborah could feel it, and the tension in her body began to flow away. She removed the challah covers, and the group murmured their appreciation of the delightful, warming smell rising from the braided loaves.

"Baruch ata adonai . . . ha-motzi lechem min ha-eretz."

They broke bread in thanks, and dinner was begun. Rebecca poured wine for everyone, and Deborah disappeared into the kitchen to turn off the oven and to bring out the salad. When she returned, Tovah was leading the group in various Shabbat songs, and David sang some Israeli folk tunes he had learned on the kibbutz where he spent the previous summer. Lev periodically joined in, or added songs from the early Workman's Circle days in his booming, accented baritone. The effect was to transport Deborah back to an earlier time, to Shabbat dinners at her grandmother's house, crammed full of aunts and uncles and cousins. It seemed to her that regardless of the level of belief, politics, or sexual orientation, all Jews had a need to gather together over food.

When Deborah, with Rabbit's assistance, brought forth the Cornish game hens stuffed with nuts and apples, her guests applauded.

"Her price is greater than rubies," Rebecca announced proudly to their guests, and Deborah's eyes shone with joy. She settled back at her seat, facing Rebecca, and they stared briefly at each other, their love obvious to everyone at the table.

"Hey, Rebecca," Greta interrupted their reverie as she passed the basmati rice, "We all know Deborah is quite the *Shaineh maidel,* but if you don't eat, we don't get to the highlight of the evening."

Rebecca turned to Greta and slowly smiled. "Oh, we will get there, don't worry," she answered.

Deborah immediately flushed, passing up the Jerusalem artichokes, even though they were her favorite. The game hen, which had tasted so tender, suddenly turned to dust in her mouth. It was really happening tonight. This Shabbat dinner was just one part of the ritual she and Rebecca had planned.

With Tovah, Saul, and Rabbit's help, Deborah finally had the table cleared, the dishes rinsed and ready in the dishwasher. They returned to the living room, where Lev led the group through an abbreviated Shabbat service, his beard and *tallis* adding to the richness of the scene. They chanted the prayers together, welcoming the evening and thanking the Creator for Shabbat and for the Torah. Then it was time to read the *parsha.* Deborah stepped forward, and the room became immediately attentive. Clearing her throat, she began the dorian cantillation of the Hebrew, the rise and fall of her voice echoing centuries of *chazzen* chanting in Poland, in Germany, in Turkey, in Chile, in Palestine, in Egypt, in all of those places where Jews had lived and studied and worshiped. The group was caught under the spell of Deborah's voice as she chanted the *parsha,* her voice finally dying away in a minor key that seemed to weep from the words. For a moment the enchantment held, then Deborah looked over at Rebecca and smiled shyly.

"Your turn," she said and, legs shaking, sat down on the arm of Greta's chair.

"My Hebrew School learning didn't stick as well with me,"

Rebecca drawled as she opened her Plaut to recite the portion in English. "I'm just going to read the part relevant to our evening's activity," she said, and Deborah felt her body shiver deliciously. Greta put her arm around Deborah as Rebecca began the reading.

"If thy brother, a Hebrew man or a Hebrew woman—I like that this portion includes women," Rebecca commented as an aside, "'be sold unto thee, he shall serve thee six years; and in the seventh year thou shalt let him go free from thee.'" Rebecca's voice was rich and full, but Deborah noticed it took on a slightly dangerously edge, as she continued with the translation. "And it shall be, if he say unto thee; 'I will not go out from thee'; because he loveth thee and thy house, because he fareth well with thee; then thou shalt take an awl, and thrust it through his ear and into the door, and he shall be thy bondsman for ever. And also unto thy bondswoman thou shalt do likewise."

Rebecca closed the book carefully and looked at the collection of people in the room. The group remained silent for a moment; then Lev began the closing blessings for the Torah service. As the "Amen" was spoken, Rebecca stood up.

"It is appropriate that we call you here on this Shabbat eve," she said. "As you all know, Deborah and I have decided to consecrate our commitment to each other tonight, with you as our witnesses and our judges. We ask your guidance, and for your blessings, as well." She then gestured to Deborah and joined Tovah on the couch. Her heart racing, Deborah rose from her perch. She looked slowly around the crowded living room: Lev in the wingback chair that, aptly, had been her father's; Benjamin, Tovah, and Rebecca on the couch; David and Saul sitting together on the loveseat; Shani stretched across its back; Rabbit sitting on the floor at her feet; Greta in the reading chair with Miriam resting on pillows nearby. Lev was right, she thought to herself. I have a *Bet Din* several times over, waiting here before me.

"The Torah portion tonight describes a way in which Jews can demonstrate their relationship to each other in a legal fashion," she began hesitantly, although she had practiced her commentary for several nights. "It is not a story of heroes, or of myths. Re-eh tells us of how regular folk—people like us, were to behave with one another. Even masters and servants."

Deborah took a deep breath. "All of you know of my relationship with Rebecca, and that she is my mistress. I am here before a *Bet Din*, and before my friends, to declare that I love my mistress and I do not wish to leave her. I make this decision of my own free will." She bowed her head, trying to slow her breathing, wondering if it was her imagination or if the room had suddenly become very warm.

"Oh, good, it's time to do the interrogation," Miriam said gleefully, sitting up and rubbing her hands together. "I say we begin with a physical inspection of the slave in question."

Greta shushed her. "In time, in time," she said. "We should check first to see if she's gone *meshuganah*, don't you think?"

Miriam pouted, but she sat back. Greta nodded to David.

"This is your department, Mr. Psychiatrist," she said. "You start."

David turned to Deborah. "Do you truly understand your desire?" David asked, his voice turning harsh. "Speak up, now." The sharpness of his voice reminded Deborah of Rebecca, and brought her nipples to a partial erection. Saul moved closer to him, as electrified by David's authority as Deborah was.

"Yes, I do," she said, watching David put his arm around his lover.

"Are you willing to submit your body and your spirit to Rebecca, to obey her completely?" David continued in the same tone.

Deborah's mind was filled with images of doing just that, so she nodded vigorously before remembering he had expected verbal responses. "Yes, I am willing," she said.

"My, she sounds eager," said Tovah. "Deborah, could you outline for us some of the duties your mistress will expect from you should you become her lifelong slave?" Her left hand was caressing Benjamin's hand, while her right was stroking Rebecca's thigh. "Go on, dear, describe to us, for instance, how you prepared for this day," she requested.

Deborah felt her knees shaking. It was embarrassing, humiliating to be put on the spot like this. But she had asked for it, had wanted it. And her cunt was beginning to fill in response to the questioning.

"I, I got up and fixed my mistress breakfast while she stayed in bed," Deborah began nervously. Tovah gave her an encouraging nod. "While she ate, I knelt at her side in case she wished anything else. We then took a shower, and I washed down her back and shampooed her hair." Tovah's hand was creeping up Rebecca's thigh, moving slowly inside, and Deborah watched her mistress smile and open her legs slightly.

"She then prepared me for my day," Deborah said, hoping that Rebecca would be distracted enough to not expect her to say more. But she was mistaken. Rebecca's half-closed eyes immediately widened and caught Deborah in their gaze.

"Tell them how I prepared you for the day," Rebecca prodded, and Deborah knew that her mistress was aware of her arousal. She could feel the blush begin to climb up her throat and warm the inside of her thighs.

"My mistress decided that I needed to, uh, clean myself, and watched while I gave myself an enema," Deborah said, her face bright red, her ass pulsing from the memory. "She then pushed a butt plug into me and had me give her sexual pleasure."

"I was horny, thinking about tonight," Rebecca explained.

Shani threw her a merry look. "Do we get details?" she asked, but Rebecca grinned and shook her head, mouthing the word "later" to Shani as the group returned its attention to Deborah.

"After my mistress was pleasured," Deborah continued, trying to ignore the fact that her nipples were pressing hard against her bra, "I was then sent shopping for tonight's dinner."

"Was the butt plug still in place?" Benjamin asked interestedly, sending a bemused glance at Rebecca and squeezing his wife's hand when Deborah blushed harder and nodded. "When I returned, I started stuffing the game hens and—"

"Wait, just a minute," Rebecca interrupted. "Didn't you forget something?" Deborah was distressed. She didn't think she would have to tell all, but apparently Rebecca expected it.

"I, I asked my mistress if I could remove the butt plug when I returned," Deborah began, her voice quivering, "but my mistress wanted me to come first." At Rebecca's warning look, Deborah continued hastily. "I mean, I was told to place nipple clamps on myself, with the chain in my mouth, and finger myself. My mistress held my head and pulled it back to tighten the chain as I got closer to—to coming." Deborah was in agony now, exposing herself so openly to her friends. "I finally came, and was permitted to remove the plug, but not the clamps."

"Are the clamps still on?" asked Greta, and she was visibly disappointed when Deborah said no.

"I took them off after I caned her," Rebecca informed the group. Immediately, Miriam clamored to see the cane marks. Deborah turned pleading eyes to Rebecca, who ignored her discomfort. "Off with the skirt, Deborah," she said. Blushing so hard it showed through her olive skin, Deborah stepped out of her skirt; she wore nothing underneath except her garter belt and a pair of tan stockings.

"Turn around, *bubeleh*," Lev requested, and, burning in shame, Deborah obeyed.

As she listened to the comments about the stripes on her ass and thighs, she felt the dampness between her legs grow, and she hoped that she would not noticeably drip as the unusual minyan continued its interrogation.

"Ah, so now we get back to the business of whether Deborah really understands what she is getting into," said David, his arm around his lover, fingers pulling at Saul's nipple absently as the young man squirmed. "Did you expect that your mistress was going to cane you?"

"I, I didn't exactly expect it," Deborah said, struggling to keep talking politely as she stood half naked, facing the group again. "I mean, I expect that my mistress will use me that way, that she will cane me or beat me as she desires. I don't always know when it's going to happen, though."

"Do you enjoy it?" Lev asked paternally. "The pain, I mean?"

Deborah nodded, feeling completely vulnerable to him and to all of them. "Speak up," Benjamin reminded her, sounding as if he was talking to one of his bar mitzvah boys. "We need your verbal replies for this to be formally accepted."

Deborah cleared her throat. "Yes," she said. "Yes, I like it in general, but I enjoy it the most when the pain is inflicted by my mistress."

That seemed to satisfy Benjamin. After a moment, Lev also sat back and sighed heavily. At the noise, the group relaxed. Rebecca requested that she remove the rest of her clothing and face the wall while they deliberated, and Deborah did so, knowing that once again the marks on her ass were exposed, but relieved that they couldn't see her face. The sense of being naked went further than her body. Having this unusual minyan listening to her describe intimate moments she shared with Rebecca, finding out how deeply she truly enjoyed submitting to Rebecca's sadism, left her feeling terribly exposed. She pressed her hot face to the wall, willing herself into a calm state, imagining herself to be that first slave so many centuries ago who endured this questioning, this exposure, because of her love for her mistress.

Finally, she was asked to turn and face them, her nakedness displayed fully to the group. Lev stood, his presence filling the room. "Our decision is that you do understand the obligations of becoming a slave for life, and that you are of sound mind in making your decision," he intoned, enjoying his role in the Bet Din. "We have also questioned your mistress and have decided that she, too, is aware of her responsibilities and obligations in such a binding relationship. And so, we have agreed to witness your physical acceptance of your newly chosen role." At his gesture, the rest of the group stood and Rebecca came forward, putting her arm around Deborah's trembling, nude body. She led Deborah to the doorway of their bedroom.

"Place your head here," Rebecca said, pointing to a space just below the mezuzah. Deborah acquiesced. Shani handed Rebecca a piercing needle and a ring. "Take three deep breaths, and let them out slowly," Rebecca ordered, and Deborah began to inhale. Greta and Miriam appeared on each side of her, holding her firmly in place. On the first inhalation she smelled rubbing alcohol and felt a cold, wet patting at her ear. On the second exhalation, she closed her eyes and heard David murmur something inaudibly. On the third exhalation, she felt a white, hot pain push its way into her left earlobe. Deborah screamed as the agonizing pain continued, the cartilage tearing its way out in front of the needle. Dimly, she felt a trickle of blood trail into her ear—and cunt juice trickle down her thigh.

"Get her a chair," Rebecca commanded, and Deborah felt her body lowered carefully onto a kitchen chair. She rested her head against the doorway, carefully avoiding the left side of her head, which was throbbing painfully.

"The ear piercing is for the world to see," Rebecca said. "This next piercing will only be shared with friends." Tovah handed Rebecca a marker and a set of surgical clamps.

"Oh, no, oh," Deborah pleaded. "I, I don't think I can—"

"Yes, you can," Rebecca answered firmly, as she made delicate marks on each side of Deborah's right nipple. The smell of alcohol revived Deborah enough to throw her close to panic. When

Rebecca pressed the steel forceps onto her erect nipple, she began to whimper. The pain she still felt in her ear was compelling her to leap away before this next needle came close to her body. Tears were streaming down her face, as Rebecca tightened the forceps, and she struggled to remain seated. When Shani handed Rebecca the second needle and ring, however, Deborah could no longer remain silent.

"Oh, mistress," she sobbed, "I am terrified I won't stay still. Please tie me down, please!"

But Rebecca shook her head. "The *Bet Din* has agreed that this piercing, too, must be of your free will." Deborah heard Lev's grunt of assent to this statement, and moaned.

"You must hold still," said Tovah. "We will hold you as best we can, but it's truly up to you." She pulled Deborah's head back by the hair, the pain clearing Deborah's mind of some of its panic. She saw David whispering into Saul's ear out of the corner of her eye, and she realized Saul was almost as frightened as she was.

"I've got to calm down, or he's going to think all lesbians are insane," she thought, and the thought made her giggle hysterically.

"Show us your strength," Rabbit's words were barely audible, but her presence revived Deborah to sanity. Deborah concentrated on slowing her breathing and counted slowly to herself. For a brief moment, she dared to admit to herself that this—the interrogation, the humiliation, the submitting to the piercing, and the pain—all of it was incredibly arousing. The clamped forceps were no longer painful, but erotic. Her terror was keeping both of her nipples rock hard. Her clit was slick from the juice of her excited cunt, and it was throbbing from the stimulation of the evening's ritual. Whatever happened next would put her over the edge. At least, Deborah hoped so.

And then—the pinching on her right nipple became unbearably intense. Pain pushed its way into her consciousness, and Deborah screamed and screamed until she was hoarse, her hands shaking with the effort of keeping her body still, of obeying her mistress, of becoming that Hebrew slave of Deuteronomy.

"Help me, help me," she cried as the needle forced its way into her body. And then the pain metamorphosed, it gripped her clit and pushed its way into her cunt like a fist and she came, in waves of orgasm, mixing pain and pleasure, transforming the terror into joy. Weeping and laughing, Deborah came again and again as the needle pushed through her flesh, pulling the ring into place. "Yes, yes," she cried hoarsely as her cunt contracted again and again.

When she was conscious again, she was lying still on the bed, wrapped in a quilt, Rabbit and Saul at her side.

"Are they in?" she asked groggily, and Rabbit nodded and kissed her.

"You were beautiful, screaming and coming," she whispered. "Even the boys were amazed."

"I was terrified," Saul admitted, and Rabbit giggled.

"Oh, he's okay," she assured Deborah. "David's teasing him about getting a PA, and I think you've given him food for thought."

"Where is everyone?" Deborah croaked, looking around vaguely.

"Oh, they're all in the dining room, eating dessert," Saul said. "We told them we'd stay with you. I kind of lost my appetite after...you know." He blushed.

"And I didn't have room after that wonderful dinner," Rabbit added. They sat quietly for a few minutes, and then Rebecca entered the room, bringing a mug of freshly brewed coffee to Deborah. Rabbit and Saul gracefully melted away as Rebecca sat next to her lover, holding the mug to her lips. After sipping a little of the fragrant brew, Deborah smiled and rested her head gingerly back against the headboard, listening to the voices of her friends floating in from the kitchen. Carefully she opened the blankets and looked down at her newly pierced nipple.

"Baruch ata adonai, elohainu melech ha-olam, shechiyanu, v'kiyamanu, vehigiyanu, lazman ha-zeh," she murmured, blissfully happy in the warmth of her mistress's arms.

"Amen," Rebecca said softly, holding her slave gently as Deborah took another sip of coffee.

La Bruja

Jenifer Levin

Over the years I'd see her sometimes, red lips, whiff of perfume, sweat on fur, smelling of Marlboros and Remy and Coke, and with sometimes-flashing, sometimes-softening eyes she'd slice a path through all those dykes to the bar. Bring the night air in. Everybody looked. But Labruja, just like royalty-she looked at no one. Then she'd sit. Her first drink always on the house.

When I watched her, the steely-shelled dark wanting deep down in me tingled every time. Along with that pull-in the hands, in the hips. Go, it said, go to her. Not that I'd dare. The fact is I was too young, too broke, too stupid. Too soft. Soft butch. Yes. Truth is the thing you never admit.

But someone older, tougher, wiser, handsome and hard like stone, dressed fine with a good tie and polished shoes and a fierce face, would appear to light her cigarette. There were still some of them around-I mean, they never really left-dykes you didn't fuck with. She'd barely touch the lighter-holding hand.

Then I would feel it drop around them both: a shining glass bubble, magnet of hearts and cunts, sealing them off from the world.

I grew. Life was not kind. Sometimes it stabbed me bad and I'd wish for the courage to die, or to kill. In the middle of despair came these dreams of Labruja. Just this picture I kept in my head of her: a walking thing of high-femme glory that no pain of the world could touch or beat out of me. All this, and I'd never even spoken to her. Yet imagined her every day. And that, just that, was a reason to go on.

Meanwhile, real life happened. I got older, smarter. Had some women and affairs. Learned how to be: how to treat women right, how to worship their hair and full painted lips. And then, later on, how to mess both up real good. Grease in your comb, on the sheets. A couple times I even fell in love-got my heart smashed, and smashed up some others. But one night after work I was having a beer and whooosh, the bar door opened to wind, burning ashes, and someone slinking by-Labruja. This time I caught her eye. That glance made me shake. And I noticed I was standing, foamy beer all over the table.

Petie yanked my jacket. "Where you think *you're* going? Child, better watch out for that witchy witch. She's high femme, high *drama*, burn you up and break you. Okay, you been warned."

By now, though, Labruja had looked away. Schlitz dripped down on my trousers, and all my friends were laughing. I shoved through elbows and thighs to find someplace more quiet. No one was fighting or kissing in the stairwell, but it smelled like piss. I let the sour dark cool off my sweat. Sometimes, there just aren't enough corners.

Got out of the bar habit and stopped going much. But one Pride Day in June, after marching and parading and pretending to die with all the fags near that church, I went to some block party downtown. I was covered with sun and dust. Sleeveless T, black jeans. I'd been working out a lot and felt good, and some pretty girls were looking. There were speakers like rocket launchers set up, everyone busy bumping with everyone else to the drumbeat blare. It was twilight. And across the street, moving slowly in an invisible circle all her own, was Labruja. Dancing. She wore a flowery, light-print dress. Not as much makeup. She'd put on weight, too, so her hips were round, breasts pressed out against cloth flowers with soft fullness. and as I pushed my way over closer I could see her skin was tight and clear, the lips full red like a heart. She'd almost lost that ragged, raw edge I remembered, looked like she was out of the life. The music stopped. Speakers crackled over the musical boom. Between buildings the sky got darker. She twirled around once more, opened her eyes. Then saw me. And smiled. I reached without thinking, took her hand like a treasure so that our palms sparked against each other's, and bent down to kiss it. "Labruja," I said, "you look beautiful."

Her eyes seemed dangerous for a second, then tender.

"Oh, honey, *call* me."

Some big dyke like a *thing* stepped in: leather boots, harsh, handsome face, pale, bloody eyes stabbing rage. "Who're you?" she said, and spun me around to face her.

Scared me at first. Then I got it together, said to myself, Addy, you are not some fucking punk. And to her, "What's the matter?"

"The lady's with me, is what." She was big, and raw-harder, wiser, tougher than me-but in that second what I saw was that she was vulnerable, hurt by the world a lot worse than I, in a way nobody could ever fix. Usually in those situations I'd back off, be a buddy, say hey, no harm intended. This time, though, her hurt fed my meanness. This time, too, was Labruja. Labruja of my dreams, getting hustled away from me now in someone else's big T-shirted arms.

So I shouted stuff after them I never otherwise would have: "Hey, you got a problem? Well fix it at home, bro'. The lady looked at *me*." And I was still shouting while they disappeared past fire hydrants and cement into shadows, when a couple other dykes grabbed both my arms, saying "Shut up kid, calm down, don't take it like this. Nice-looking kid like you, you'll get your own woman some day-Labruja's with Mick now, understand? She is Mick's. That's all."

More years passed. I got to feeling good in an older, grown-up way, and I was just about cock of the walk late one spring-time afternoon, stepping out of work early and down to the gym to lift hard, do sit-ups, biceps, get pumped, that nice rush and the so-fine scent and flesh swell after shower, after towel-down. Bag of wet sweats in one hand, I was on the street whistling, breeze in the air, my shoes very shined. Remembering this rumor someone had passed on to me the other night: *Now's your chance, sweets. Mick left the bitch!* Well, I was ready. Old enough. Tough enough. Handsome enough. Had a job. Paid my own way. No major fuck-ups. No, no more. Just one more fine stud bouncing down a breezy springtime city street, quarters in my palm, heading for the nearest pay phone. This time I'd do it. Call that Labruja. This time, she'd be mine.

First phone had the receiver ripped out. But I maintained what you'd call serenity. Another corner. Quarter went in and I was whistling, heart thumping, waiting and waiting, but no dial tone. I banged it a couple times with my fist, but nothing slid back. Now there was one quarter left. So I headed for another bunch of phones a block away, my mouth dry and sweat starting at the roots of my hair. This one had a dial tone. I put in the quarter, punched all the right buttons.

Then a woman-I'd seen her here and there at some places, maybe, only now she was walking with a little boy of about three-brushed past. The kid got in her way and she tripped, dropped two brown bags of groceries at my feet. A catsup bottle smashed, mayonnaise splattered-all over my shoes. The kid fell on his knees, and he was crying.

"Shit!" I yelled.

"Oh God, sorry!" she yelled, and started to cry, too. I let the receiver dangle, stooped to help with their fucking groceries. The kid was really screaming. She was sobbing something about how it's food or rent and what the fuck was she gonna do now. I helped her pick up bruised apples, a box of smashed eggs. Out on the Drive it was rush hour, major traffic tie-up. Cars waiting at exits spewed and honked. My breezy springtime city turned into a whirling circle of chaos and sound, and in the center of it I was helping some bitch and her brat pick up their ruined groceries while the receiver of my dreams dangled close by, and I was ignoring a phone call I'd waited my whole life to make.

I stood covered with foodstuffs. Pressed the phone to my ear. Hello, I said, vacantly. Maybe Labruja had answered it before, but now it was dead. I set it quietly back on the hook.

Sometimes gentlemanhood takes over. I let it do that with this grocery bitch and kid. Wiped off cans and bottles. Crammed as much stuff as I could into my gym bag.

"Here," I said dully, "I'll help you home."

"Gee," she sniffled, "that'd be great."

I pulled out some gum and gave it to the kid to shut him up. He paused with it halfway to his mouth, stared tear-stained and imploring up at her.

"Go on, sweetheart, you could have it."

Her voice was tender.

He was soft brown like her, with somebody else's eyes.

We walked slowly as he toddled along chewing happily, away from park and Drive, shortcutting through the projects. Past a couple dumpsters, brick, concrete. She lived up some flights, and in the dim light when we paused on landings I saw that she was not beautiful, really, but sweet, with a shining on her cheeks and way down deep in the eyes that told me yes, she was kind.

Her place was a little cozy crazy bright hole, plant-littered, toy-littered, that sucked you right in and made you want to stay. I helped her unload crushed containers of food, watched as she put them away. Just as I was about to leave, the kid had to go potty. I waited while she mopped up his rear end. He seemed happy now, so I gave him another piece of gum.

"Take off your shoes," she said. "I'm real sorry, I'll clean them."

She set my shoes on newspaper, pulled out a cloth and brush

and buffer, black polish, rags. I sat on her sofa barefoot, watching. How she bent gently over those shoes, with humility and care. How her fingers were gentle and strong. The kid sat on my lap, just like that.

"He likes you." She offered up the shoes. Taking them, I touched her wrist. Skin rubbed. Eyes met. "Hey," she said softly, "you wanna stay for dinner?"

"Okay," I told her.

But it was like I wasn't in charge of my own voice. Some ache inside of me spoke instead, a deep sore aching mixed with quiet calm mixed with a desire that I hadn't even known I'd had, but I could feel without knowing, somehow, that here, in here-if I stayed-she might ease it.

So I stayed.

I never really left.

That was Rosa.

More years passed. Things with me, Rosa, and the kid were great. If we had problems, we'd work them through. I didn't have much to complain about. At night sometimes she'd just touch and pull me in, her femmeness and hunger washing over me with every move of her soft woman body. What I had with them gave me a warm, strong, solid core inside. But the warmth lived right next to a darkness. It was the other part of me, the part of dream and unquenchable desire: a hard, persistent, shadowy butch thing that left me always restless, always somehow far away from what I loved and had. I kept that part pretty quiet. Most times, didn't even touch on it myself. Things were too damn good.

One cold late winter in the middle of all this wonderfulness, the kid had a vacation and she decided they gotta go to Miami and see his grandma. She and he will fly super-saver; four days later come back to me. I helped them pack. Kissed and hugged them good-bye. Put them on the bus to LaGuardia. Missed them.

"Yo," said Petie later that night, on the phone, "you heard?"

"Heard what?"

"Shit. Labruja. She's at St. Vincent's. She's dying."

"Whaddaya mean, dying?"

"I mean like, *dying*. I mean, I guess the life caught up with her."

I worked out hard at the gym. Picked up a video on my way home. In the kid's room I turned down his blanket, just so, the way I did every night, so that the bed was waiting for him-even though they wouldn't be back for days. I got to sleep around midnight. There were voices in my dream. *Child*, they said, *your heart is your own.*

Next morning was Saturday. I bathed and dressed, combed and polished to kill. Money in the pocket. And rubbers. I was packing, for the first time in years. The cock buckled on with leather sat there with its base above my cunt, the rest of it strapped back between my thighs, a faint bulge swelling out against my baggy jeans crotch. It was unfamiliar for a minute or two, my walking clumsy, self-conscious; then I got the rhythm, then I had the power, power of a dream, power of a lover, and I walked outside so sure of dreams and of the realness and power of desire, for the first time in forever.

It was cold, streets and trees bare, the wind blowing garbage around an early weekend morning stuck in the winter chill between snows. I stopped at the Korean guy's fruit stand and stared at the roses. One stood alone, silvery-soft, naked, strange, like shaped metal on fire.

"I'll take that one there."

"That platinum rose. Rare, only one left, ten bucks."

I didn't argue. Made sure he wrapped the stem and tied it with white ribbon. Then, holding it close, I hailed a cab heading west.

"St. Vincent's," I said, "off of Seventh."

They gave me a pass at the desk. I was up elevators and down halls, dodging wheelchairs and carts. Peeking around the corner of a dark room. Thumping heart. Shy.

"Labruja. You remember me?"

She was propped on pillows, her makeup fresh. "Addy, honey," she said smiling, "of course!" and offered a hand, very gracious. I took it gently, turned it to kiss. Ran a finger over it and could feel veins. I sat on the side of the bed and sensed for a second the sharp knob of a knee against my back. She moved it discreetly away with a faint swish of white sheet.

I noticed bouquets and vases of flowers, cards and presents on the little table next to her bed. They were all pretty, all expensive, crowding one another out. Too many for the nightstand to contain. Then I looked down at the single, dumb little rose in my hand and felt small for a second, shabby, still too young for her somehow. The lady had plenty of friends and admirers. She hadn't exactly been waiting for me all these years. But I offered it anyway.

"Here, every pretty girl deserves flowers."

This made it almost okay. Labruja held it to her cheek a second.

Then guided my chilled hand to her nose, mouth, and cheek and breathed deep.

"God, you smell like outside! Like the air, I mean, like the world. Oh, it smells so good!"

"You can't die, Labruja," I blurted. "Because of women like you, I never killed myself." I sat back and apart then, my fingers suddenly clumsy without hers. Surprised because I had no idea that's what I felt or would say, but there, there it was, and it was true.

She gave a little gasp. And cried. The tears made mascara-edged rivers through rouge, powder, foundation. I dabbed at them with a hanky.

We talked some, quietly. Shyly at first. About her life. Mine. We'd never really spoken much before. Then she lay back on the pillows, very tired, and took my hand in hers again.

"I want to run away," she said, sadly, "but I can't."

Already an idea was ringing in my head. I reached through bouquets for the phone.

"Yes you can," I said. "Let me take you."

After the call I turned away while she dressed. I found her coat in a closet near the bed. It was long, long-sleeved, covered the hospital ID around her wrist. Then we were walking slowly, casually, around hallway carts and wheelchairs and trays of unclaimed lunch, through the antiseptic smell, avoiding nurses' eyes. And down. In a dream haze. And out-on the street, among cabs, in the cold. Tears came to her but didn't flow. A taxi stopped and I opened the door. Trembling, I helped her inside.

"Uptown," I said. "To the Waldorf-Astoria."

Rich people's hotel lobbies are all carpets and glass, lights, terra cotta, gold, and everyone bustling silently. No, they are not silent but muffled, muted, their voices refined and footsteps hushed. So that's how it was: the whole big rich unfamiliar place surrounded me and her, but we moved forward through it in the same warm protective bubble that had carried us this far. I sat her down on a chair.

Petie met me, eyes darting everywhere, all done up in his uniform of wine-scarlet with bright gold tassels. The little hat brim over his face, sort of ridiculous, and at the same time all business. He spoke without looking at me, nervous, and handed over the keys.

"Twelfth floor, number 1285. You got until noon tomorrow. Then the next shift comes on and it's scheduled to clean." His voice had gone husky, there was stubble on both cheeks. I figured he was on the juice again. Personally, I wouldn't touch that stuff, but it was none of my business anyway.

"Thanks," I muttered, sweating.

And keys in hand, I floated across the carpet like I belonged there with all the muffled, smart-dressed servants and guests, to the soft, plush lobby chair where Labruja sat next to a mound of someone else's high-polished leather luggage, pale and waiting, half a smile on her lips. I offered my arm. Very gentlemanly. And together we traveled to the row of silently blinking elevator buttons. Out of the sides of their eyes people glanced at us sometimes, glanced again, seemed puzzled, turned heads ever so slightly to stare in that discreet don't-ask way of the wealthy and polite. Something in the eyes turned hard and self-satisfied once they'd seen that yes, we both were women, and no, we could not fool them. Poor straights. They'd be disappointed if they'd known that I didn't even want to-fool them, that is. I was too far away from their life to try, and the woman on my arm took me farther. So we waited, Labruja and I, and we floated up together noiselessly in the glass-shining, brass-shining elevator. Down hallways with carpets that absorbed our feet. Where the lighting was delicate, kind on her exhausted face and eyes. Where the shake of her hand and the flush of her fever was hidden, known only to me now, and I held the shake of her and the flush of her in my own hands and heart.

"Labruja," I said. Just that-her name.

And opened the door.

Silent flick of a light switch. The carpets, smooth walls, sparkling polish of things. Plush sofa and chairs. Gilt-edged mirror. Heavy, thick drapes to pull across windows sparkling out on city skyline. A little pint-sized refrigerator stocked with snacks wrapped in pretty French and English packages. A bar with every kind of fancy booze under the sun. All these things were there for us. Maybe Petie'd kill me later, but I had to try stuff out. Poured spring water for the lady-she couldn't stomach anything else, she said-and popped a soda can for me. Sure, I thought about champagne. But Labruja wasn't drinking hard stuff, not any more. I decided maybe I wouldn't either.

She was like a kid for a while, asking me to bring her things to look at: the room service menus, the special thick glossy entertainment magazines. Me? I was a willing servant. In between doing what she bid, bringing hotel knickknacks to her, taking them back to their places, I sat next to her on the sofa fingering velveteen and cushions, and we talked. We talked the afternoon away. Flicked on the TV-cable-with a multipurpose smooth-buttoned remote. There'd been a scent to her when we came in, I realized. Hospital disinfectant, alcohol swabs, very medicinal. Now, though, it was gone. She turned the TV off. Talked some more, this time about Mick. The first thing that brought them together, she said: Mick was strong.

I didn't know whether to believe her or not.

"I want to feel someone strong again," she said. "I think I'd like to feel you that way, strong and alive."

I'd only been waiting my entire life.

I leaned over closer to her heat and fever. Then I just pulled her up and onto me. Her legs and arms wrapped around, riding.

I rested against a wall, holding her. She was frail, child-light, so easily supported. I moved my hands on her ass and thighs slowly, pressing her down, moved my hips up into pure woman smell and nylon. That's when she felt it for the first time, and breathed out once, loud, surprised, "*God*, hon'."

The bed was king-size, pillow-littered, a vast thing to get lost on. I rolled over it into her mouth and hair. She pressed finger-nails against my neck. Then something fierce got me moving on top of her so hard and blurred and fast I forgot who I was, and I pulled back for a moment, blinking, when she called out in pain. She made one great effort then, pushed me down by the shoulders. Crawled on top of me, very graceful, older, wiser, knowing and smiling, rubbing against my thighs and belt.

"Stay still, hon'." She pushed off my jacket. Unbuttoned my shirt, pulled the tails of it out to each side, unbuckled my belt and teased down a zipper, then briefs, then reached between my legs, and the cock sprang rubbery free.

"Mmmm-mmmm. That for me?"

"Yes, baby."

"Well," she said, "I got a present for you, too." She went into one of my pockets and pulled out a rubber, and the plastic wrapping crackled. I reached. "Uh-uh," she said, "let me." With one expert motion it was on, little waiting bubble at the tip for a sperm that does not exist except in the hard strong make-believe love-fucking of the mind. She rolled to one side and peeled her nylons off. Then crouched over me again in nothing but the dress, and came down on top of me, slowly, while I guided the cock inside.

"Aaah," she sobbed, hurting, and took it all in. Then just sat on it and on me breathing fast, tears streaming. I reached up under soft flaps of dress to hold her hips. Ran my thumbs across her belly, across all the bumps of scars.

"They cut everything out of me, hon'."

I licked one finger, touched it to her clit, and she moaned. "Not everything."

"Be soft, hon'," she said "Go slow."

I rocked up into her with a sure, smooth motion that made her lips part and eyes flick shut, then open, made her smile sweet. It was something that in my daydreams I always meant for her to feel. Meant for her to know just who and what I could be for her here, in this room, in this place, in the shadows, just for her: a lover who knew how to wait, and knew how to move, to hold back, give, fuck, caress, take, a woman who was old enough and ready enough, tough enough, soft enough, wise enough now, and in love. Who had come to find her still alive—finally, yes, and not a moment too late.

Sometime during that afternoon we had all our clothes off, strewn over floor and bedcovers like unnecessary things, and in the heavy, peaceful curtain-drawn quiet lay side by side on damp sheets, half asleep. I was totally naked, not even packing. She ran a hand in circles on my belly.

"So smooth. Mine's ruined."

"No, baby."

"Mick never let me touch her."

"Hmmm. But you wanted to?"

"Oh," she mumbled, suddenly shy, "yeah. Sometimes. What about you with your lady? You let her touch you?"

"Well, sure, sometimes."

"*You soft*," she teased. Then, very serious, "See, stay that way. Stay nice and strong and soft for your lady. Stay good to her."

Then she slid a finger inside me without even asking, and something escaped from my mouth, a piece of my guts, like a breath or a sound. What all the surgery had left criss-crossed her belly, a dark red death messenger. Platinum petals. But the rest of her was still alive, her hands and eyes seeking life.

"You just *let* me," she whispered fiercely. "Stay right there, like so. Give it to me. Give it to me. Give it to me, honey."

I showered in a bathroom like a palace. Later I cleared marble shelves of all the special little containers of shampoos and conditioners and stuffed them into a bag.

When I drifted out with the steam she was dressed. Feverish, weaker than ever, but sitting there in the quiet-draped dark, smiling. She hadn't bathed. "I want to smell like today," she said, "for as long as possible."

I left the key and a ten on the dresser. Big spender. But in the elevator all that floating peace inside started to be pulled down, pushed apart, like shattered glass, ruined light. Grace and mercy left me. I had no idea what time it was. Stepping out into the cold of a bitter winter weekend night told me it was late, and my insides went desolate. A cab stopped and the hotel hop opened a door for Labruja. I gave him a couple bucks. Watching her fold herself slowly, achingly inside, I knew for sure then how weak she was, how little time she had, so when I climbed in after her I sent all the bad fear feelings inside me away and pressed her hands between mine. "St. Vincent's," I told the guy, "downtown, take Seventh. And please take it easy, the lady doesn't feel good."

"I'm sorry," he said, "no problem."

Shampoos rattled in her purse.

"Should I call you?" I whispered.

"No, I don't think so, hon'."

We were silent. But partway downtown in that cab on that night-lit city avenue we turned to each other, suddenly laughing. Roaring. It came from deep in the gut, warm, delicious, spiced like life. I understood then that this was the last time I'd ever see her, my desire and dream, my Labruja. Because somehow she was mine. Oh, sure, maybe other people's, too. But also mine in a way that she'd never been before. And as long as I lived-which, for sure, would be longer than she did-I could have her this way.

At the hospital's main entrance we were both still smiling. I got out to open her door. She staggered by, utterly exhausted, but with a fiery look to her, brushed my cheek with her lips. I watched her walk unsteadily away. She waved once without turning. Last I saw she'd taken out the platinum rose, which was wilted with cold and crushed, but she was holding it to her nose, breathing deeply. She was entering the lobby, her patient wristband showing from beneath a coat sleeve. She turned once to blow me a kiss. Then entered the revolving door of shadows and of glass, dancing, reeling on feverish feet, spinning 'round and 'round.

A couple days later Rosa and the kid came back. I met them at LaGuardia. We went home together in the bus.

The kid was happy because he got some toys and shit from his cousins. Rosa looked great. Said it was good to see everyone but she'd missed me. "Yeah," I said, "I missed you too." Then she was quiet.

That night we fixed spaghetti with meatballs. I made tomato sauce from scratch. The kid helped, stirring in onions. And our whole place got that warm home family air, covering us all in a kind of blanket of closeness, familiarity, and affection. We ate, caught a couple shows on TV. Bathed the kid, tucked him into bed, and it was my turn to read a story. Later I headed for the kitchen to help clean up and found myself drying dishes.

"Coffee?" Rosa took out the can. I said, "Sure."

"Tried calling you the other night," she said. "You weren't home."

"Huh," I mumbled, "which night?"

"Oh," she said, "the one before last."

I was glad she couldn't see me. But gentlemanhood kicked in fast and helped me save my sorry butt. I stayed right on my toes. "Oh," I said, very casual, "that. Well, I was pretty beat, baby. I just turned in early, must of turned off the phone."

"Ah."

Soon the coffee was bubbling away, filling the warm kitchen with a homey, fine perfume.

"You know," she said, "Angie called the day before I left. She told me something about that ho', you know, the one used to go with Mick? Well, she said the bitch is dying."

"Uh-huh," I said. "No kidding?"

Then before I knew it an almost-full can of El Pico came sailing through the air, bounced off the kitchen cabinet leaving a big scarry dent in wood, just about an inch above my head. It crashed into the sink, and I wheeled around to face her.

"What the fuck!"

Her face was burning, eyes and mouth anguished slits. "That," she hissed, "that's for turning off the phone."

I spent a few nights on the couch.

Winter slowed us down.

Springtime the kid was doing great at school, Rosa got back to her old sweet ways, I kept up pretty steady at the gym. Since that one night, no more coffee cans got tossed my way.

I heard through the grapevine that so-and-so was with so-and-so, and this one had left that one to go there-fucking dykes and their affairs, you know, all of us hopping around on this board of a city like a bunch of Chinese checkers. In my heart center settled that big sure steadiness again: Rosa, and me, and the kid.

Desire is something with a mind and a heart of its own. It picks us up, spins us around in the brilliant cloud world of extreme unction, crisis times, life and death, a soul-world of always-passion, gold hotels, and dreams. Then it spits you out real good. Me? Like most folks, I move most times in the touchable, nondream, material world of real things: a job, a home, a woman and child. Just me. In all my soft butchness, hard womanness, all my heart's truth and lies. Nobody's savior. Nobody's angel.

Labruja died that spring. They had a service at the Community Center. I heard that Mick cried.

One afternoon, weeks later, I was lying near the window in our bedroom after work, waiting for Rosa and the kid to come home. A leaf blew past the fire escape, riding on what looked like a puff of something thicker than air, like silver smoke. I saw it through the turned-up blinds. And I thought: Desire. Petals. Labruja.

My woman and kid, they are so real. Kindness. Anger. Love. What I need, for my life. And I am what they need, too. This I know, deep down inside.

But I've got this other desire inside for things that don't have a whole hell of a lot to do with the life that happens to me, to most of us I guess, day after day. Call it crazy butch dreaming-Petie does. The hard, buried part. The not-woman, not-man, just-butch darkness in me. That could love and want Labruja.

See, she was real, too. Not what I needed-but what I wanted. What I almost never grew up enough for.

The leaf blew by. Puff of smoke. Lipstick trace. A dream. Lucky me. To get, in life, what I wanted. And to also give back something. And, no matter how many cans of El Pico go sailing past my head, to be smart enough to shut up about it.

Femmes. They're a mystery to me. Mine, or hers, or yours-oh, we think we're so tough, but none of us ever own them. Yet among them sometimes are the ones that just looking at keeps your dreams alive, so you can go on surviving yourself. It's this passion they have for what you are in your own butch heart. It never dies in them-it's something you can count on. Keeps you going when you'd rather not. It caresses you free of shame. So no matter who you love in everyday life, you will never stop dreaming of them. Every living day. Gods or goddesses or demons give me this: my dream femmes, these special tender women whom you want without end but also somehow without selfishness. I mean, without coveting. See, women to me are love. Also, desire. But that's not all they are.

Alone, I'm mostly my own butch shadow. Watching the drift. Wanting the dream. Inside the shadow, desire rises. Then the magic. And love. All but unspoken. Says one word, one yearning, a name. Always and forever to me-Labruja.

Some women, you're glad they've lived. And not just for yourself.

Virgin's Gift

Robin Bernstein

Anat skipped school again today. I know she's waiting for me on the roof of the movie theater, chalking Hebrew obscenities in the tar and watching the traffic below. I know she's waiting for me.

"Hey, Baby, what took you so long?"

That's what she'll ask, if I meet her on the roof. I'll pull myself over the rail, rust from the fire escape streaking my hands and face. Before I can even wipe the dirt away, though, Anat will whip my long hair out of my face and kiss my lips. Kiss them deeply. And then demand more.

But I'm not going to the roof, at least not yet. I'm going to Rosenbloom's Jewish Books and Religious Articles. To buy Anat a present.

My sneakers beat a rhythm on the sidewalk as questions pound through my head. Who is this girl who thrust herself into my life only a few weeks ago? Why should I buy her a present, when she bosses me around, makes fun of my lack of experience, and never answers a direct question? My answers also resound in rhythm:

I'll buy her a present to make her miss Israel less, so she'll be less moody-and less likely to take it out on me. I'll buy her a present to apologize for not sleeping with her yet. To bribe her to wait for me. To make her want me even more.

A bell jingles when I open the door to Rosenbloom's. The Hasid at the counter looks up at me, then immediately looks away. For a moment I feel rude in my jeans and grungy turtle-neck-hardly yeshiva-girl regulation. There's something in the Bible about women not wearing pants, like you're not supposed to confuse the genders or something. The Hasid's contempt is almost palpable. *Screw you,* I think, *I'm just as Jewish as you are. I've got as much right to be here.* Well, maybe I don't. It is his store.

I want to buy Anat something cute, like a Hebrew picture book or stencil set or refrigerator magnet or something. But I get distracted by the silver in the locked glass cases: heavy, shining candlesticks; ornate little boxes with hinged lids; menorahs whose graceful, twisting tines resemble flame itself, frozen mid-flicker. The weight of each piece crushes ridges into the velvet shelves. A Hasidic woman is behind me, digging through a trough of yarmulkes. She is in her thirties, wearing a soft, sacklike hat, calf-length blue skirt, and white tights, like every other Hasidic woman I've ever seen. She picks up a yarmulke, inspects it from all sides, tugs at the seams, peers, sneers, and tosses it back. She already has six or seven in her fist: one sedate black disk and a bunch of bright preschool-size yarmulkes with logos from foot-ball teams and Sesame Street. I wonder how many sons she has. I wonder who her husband is.

Suddenly, my mouth and eyes are wet. *It must be so easy,* I think. Longing splashes all over me, sudden as thunder and rain. To be this Hasidic woman, to have my life set: husband, sons, buying yarmulkes on a Wednesday afternoon. So easy. So clear. She doesn't have to ghost her way through high school, laboring each day to remain as inconspicuous as possible. She's not so lonely that she'll settle for anyone-even a sullen semidelinquent who thinks all Americans are idiots-just to have someone to talk to. She would never be on her knees in gratitude, buying a girl a present just so she'll stick around. And when this Hasidic woman has sex-which she does, and I don't-she does it in a clean bed with the door closed. Not on a dirty roof with the sun beating down.

Oh, you're idealizing, I chide myself. She probably works twenty hours a day, boiling chickens and wiping baby butts. And what if she's lesbian, too? Imagine how awful that would be, to have to marry some guy or lose your whole community.

But maybe she's never even heard of lesbians. Then, maybe, it wouldn't be so bad. Would I be able to imagine women together, if I'd never heard the words? Maybe I'd think I was just shy or asexual. Maybe it would even be sort of okay.

I imagine myself, Hasidic, in bed, waiting for my husband. He pulls back the covers and climbs in-

No. The fantasy doesn't work; I'm cold as the silver behind the glass. I can't have this life, even in dreams.

The Hasidic woman has noticed my stare; she's sizing me up me out of the corner of her eye. I move to the racks of tallises: dazzling white linen with silk embroidery, dark stripes and soft fringes. They have so much.

What if she *is* straight? I look at the Hasidic woman again. Imagine how wonderful that would be, to share desire with one person, over and over. I guess some Hasidic women don't love their husbands. But imagine being one of the ones who does. Imagine wanting your husband, never worrying about whether it was right or normal or if you were really sure or if you might change your mind. Never worrying about what anyone might think; knowing that everyone-family, friends, neighbors, rabbi, God Himself-was urging every kiss, every moan, every tremor in your hips. Imagine wanting your husband, wanting him, only him. And having him, over and over, year after year. Limitless.

I imagine myself not only Hasidic, but straight. Touching my husband, clinging to him, opening myself to him-

No. It still doesn't work. I can't enter this image, can't access this joy. So many people have it, and I never will.

I turn to the racks of books. I can always lose myself in words, in that march of black letters across white pages. Regular and fixed.

But these books offer no such escape. The books in these racks are heavy, bound in soft leather and stamped in gold. I can't read the Hebrew, but I know they're prayer books. Or the Talmud. Or other stuff so holy I've never even heard of it. Heavy, beautiful books over which men run loving fingers, straining their eyes and pursing their murmuring lips. Books that are cherished, held and kissed, protected and praised. I wish someone would hold me, bless me, open me, read me, love me as each of these books will be. Each of these racks and racks of books that never need to be anything but what they are.

And I wish I could love these books the way the men do. Anat could read these pages, but I don't think she could tremble with them, cry as I've seen men cry. She doesn't care about religion, probably wouldn't be impressed by the soft leather covers and gold-rimmed leaves.

I'm tired of being unimpressed, of not caring. I wish love would flow out of me like it flows from the quaking men in synagogue. I wish I believed in God. I wish I could love leather-bound books and God with all my soul, with all my passion, with no hesitancy or self-consciousness or shame. I wish I could love a girl with my heart and my eyes and my lips; a girl who'd accept my love without laughing at me or calling me a stupid American virgin or wanting to pound my hips into the tar on a filthy roof. I wish I could love easily, fully, three times a day in synagogue and every night in a clean bed with my wife-

I stop short. *My wife?* That's not what I meant. Wives are for-

I grab a book and leaf through it, trying to remember my Hebrew alphabet, trying to recognize a word or two, trying to concentrate. Trying to push away the idea that has already exploded into countless streaks of light like fireworks and now buzzes toward me from every direction, unavoidable-

If I were a man.

If I were a man. A Hasid. I could love my wife, over and over, year after year, limitlessly.

I almost put the book down and run from the store. *Oh no, I think, does this mean I'm a transsexual? Please, please, I pray to a god I don't believe in, not that. I have so many problems already.*

But the idea still pulses through me, the image of myself as a Hasid. Loving a woman over and over, with all the blessings of the fathers.

I turn again to the Hasidic woman. She has finished selecting yarmulkes and has migrated toward the cash register. I imagine myself touching her, knowing she has never been touched by any man-not at all, not even a handshake-other than her husband.

Knowing her breasts-her stomach, her shoulders, maybe even her *wrists*-have never been seen by any man except her husband. Imagining myself as that husband, imagining a woman so honoring me. Sharing her body with me, only me, forever.

But this woman is not my type. She's as old as my mother, for one thing. And her hands are full of yarmulkes for her husband and sons. There is no room for me in that bed. I need my own wife to love.

I rush to a rack of lucite key rings with women's names. My wife must have a name. (*My wife*-the thought still terrifies me, but I will not think now about what it might mean.) I flip through the plastic tags: Yocheved, Malka, Ruchel-I don't like these names. What are the Hasidic girls on my block called? Gitti, Shoshana, Chanie-That's the one. But not Chanie. Chana. My wife is named Chana.

My wife.

Chana.

The wedding guests are still dancing, men waving bottles of wine and schnapps on one side of the hall, women on the other side weaving through circles of dance and gossip. My father and uncles pushed me into a chair, then raised it above their heads and bounced me toward the ceiling to the sound of accordions and fiddles. After the women did the same with Chana, my parents and her parents were also danced through the air. Then my father brought me another shot of schnapps and told me to leave the party. My time had come.

So now I am home with my Chana. Now I am in the bedroom I will share always with Chana.

A man is not supposed to look at a woman unless she is his wife. As a boy, of course, I looked into the faces of my mother and sisters. But as I grew older, I learned to look at the ground or at other men when women passed. In moments of weakness I have snuck quick glances-haven't we all?-but I have never held a woman's gaze. Now, for the first time, I may look. Without fear. Without shame. For as long as I want. Without pretending to do otherwise. Without disguising my passion.

Her eyes are as hungry as mine; her gaze darts over every point of my face. Unmarried women must keep a distance from men as well, if they want to retain respect. But now, we may both look, and we do, we do.

And my eyes...how can I see so much at once? Her long face, full lips, soft gray eyes-so much to see. The vast expanse of skin from forehead to chin, from nose to ear on each side. So much exposed. So much softness. And I will touch that softness tonight, and over and over for the rest of my life. I am weak with unbelieving.

She removes the veil covering the top of her head, and her curly hair falls down. As a married woman, she will cover her hair in public from now on, but she will not shave her head as women used to. We are a modern people. Chana's black curls tumble around her face; the smell of shampoo drifts toward me.

For a moment, my amazement is displaced by panic. Who is this woman who has been thrust into my life? Ours was not purely an arranged marriage; we have spoken several times and consented to each other. But one could not say we know each other well. Perhaps we should not touch tonight, but instead talk.

Chana has noticed the distraction in my eyes; questions and disappointment fog her face.

I push my hesitancies aside. Tomorrow we will talk. We have the expanse of our whole lives to get to know each other. Tonight we must fulfill our obligation to each other, not as individuals but as man and woman, husband and wife. Tonight, we exist only to satisfy each other's desire, as we have been commanded.

Without thinking, I reach out my hand to her. She raises her hand and lays a single finger in my palm. We sit on the bed together, the pad of her finger slowly tracing lines in my palm. I am transfixed by her finger, by skin touching skin. Somehow, I never believed I could really be so lucky. I never thought this would actually happen to me.

I close my hand around her finger and press hard. I hear her breath catch and I look up, concerned that I have hurt her. But her lips are parted, eyes half-closed, cheeks flushed.

The sight ignites me so. I grab both her hands in mine, and without even thinking, I am kissing them, rubbing my lips feverishly against her palms, licking the cracks between her fingers.

Chana is moaning now. I take each manicured finger full in my mouth, sucking hard. She rakes her nails through my beard. I lick, suck, bite, breathe hot over her wrists, feel her pulse through my lips. Chana is gasping now and maybe I am, too. I slide off the bed and kneel before her, hugging her hands to the sides of my head, blocking out our sounds. It's too much. I can't take it all in one night.

But Chana will not let me escape. Still in her wedding gown, she slides off the bed and kneels beside me on the floor. The dress rustles as if layers hid beneath the skirt.

My hands still clasp hers tight to the sides of my head. But suddenly, she takes control and pulls my face toward hers. And

Chana, my Chana, kisses me full on the lips.

Oh, so many times I have praised God, so many nights I have recited the *shma*, the call to all Jews on Earth. *Shma Yisroel Adonai Elohenu Adonai Echad*-Hear, oh Israel, the Lord is God, the Lord is One. But only when Chana's soft lips meet mine, when I taste her breath and feel the flicker of her tongue-only then, for the first time, do I feel my spirit burst from my body to touch all others. Only this joyful noise could reach all on earth. This kiss is the *shma*-hear oh Israel, this kiss is God, and we are one. Chana and I. And all Jews, *shma*, all breathing creatures on the earth, *shma*, all kisses, *shma*, are one.

We fall to the floor.

Chana is in my arms and we are rolling. I'm so happy, I start to laugh. For a moment, she looks confused, then she laughs, too, grabbing me tighter as we roll on the carpet. It feels so good, this squeezing. All these years of not being touched; now I press her hard against my chest, kissing and laughing, rolling and gazing and laughing for a long, long time.

But suddenly, through our laughter, I become aware of her breasts pressing against my chest like two soft biscuits. And my laughter dissolves.

Something serious sweeps through me-a new kind of grave desire incinerating my bones, my flesh, my thinking mind. My laughter is gone; I hold Chana tense, my eyes inches from hers. And she stops laughing, too.

"Chana," I say, my voice so smoked with desire that I barely recognize it. "Chana," I say, "Please take off your dress."

She is still for a moment. Her eyes close once, then open to me. She kisses me once more, quickly, on my lips. And then she pulls away.

"Yes," she says, and the word sounds like a single drop of rain sliding off a leaf. "Yes, I will take off my dress for you."

And wonder of wonder, it happens. Chana stands without breaking my gaze. Watching my eyes, she reaches around to her own back in a way I did not know arms could bend. And she slowly unzips her wedding gown. Then she loosens the cuffs around her wrists. And slowly, as if by magic, the dress sinks to the floor. The white dress is heaped around Chana's ankles, like clouds at the feet of God. I am worshiping.

Do all women have so much skin beneath their clothes? The thought is incredible, obscene. No wonder men and women are separated so strictly; what man could concentrate enough to tie his own shoes with women hovering about, half-naked and entrancing, hidden only by thin sheaths of cloth?

But now I do not need to concentrate on anything but my Chana, who stands before me in white underpants and a brassiere. Chana, with the bony, pale shoulders, the impossible softness tucked into her brassiere, the small roundness of her belly.

"And you?" she whispers.

"What?"

"My husband," she says, "take off your suit."

For a moment, I am shocked. In anticipation of this night, I had imagined touching Chana, imagined us pushing together beneath the covers. But it never occurred to me that I might undress in front of her. I am suddenly sheepish. My clothes will not curl gracefully from my body as hers did from her; I doubt I could muster the power to stand unclothed and commanding as she. I cannot equal her, can never be as beautiful for her as she is for me.

Her beauty is a gift I must accept humbly, knowing I can never return it.

But she is my wife. And she is right. I must satisfy her tonight. And she wants me naked before her. So be it.

I stumble to my feet and begin tugging at my shirt. My fingers, so sensitive a moment ago, now struggle. It's as if the buttons had turned to mist; I can't grip them. But finally I release myself. The trousers are easier; they unzip like Chana's dress. I kick them aside.

I stand in my underwear, undershirt, and tallis. Do I take off the prayer shawl? I suppose I must. I lift it off gingerly, suppressing an urge to flick the fringes against her belly. I fold my tallis neatly on the nightstand.

"Undershirt, too," she says. There is no graceful way to obey; I yank the shirt over my head.

And we stand, three feet of air pulsing between us. She gapes at the hair on my chest-Is it enough? Is it too much? I worry-and on my stomach. I feel each hair spring to life and reach toward her, like the fur on a jungle cat's back.

And Chana, my Chana, moves toward me.

But she stops, inches away. I can see every pore, every freckle on her shoulders. She smells like soap and wine and something else I've never smelled before. I want her all at once, hot and electric, inside and outside, I want her so badly, now and forever, I want her so, I almost cry with the wanting. I almost fall to my knees and cry. No one has ever before had such power over me; at this moment, I would trade my soul, sell myself into bondage for her. And at the same time, my desire could burst from my body, grip her, deliver her to me like a wave crashing on the shore. I am a king about to devour a feast. I am a boy afraid to taste the wine.

I move not at all.

Slowly, sighing, Chana folds herself into me. First she touches her bare shoulder to mine. Then she rolls her bosom against my chest. And her silken hands slide to my back.

So much warm skin against skin.

My hands travel up and down her spine. And through the curls of her hair.

Now our kisses come fast, forcefully. I kiss through the softness of our lips, into the hardness of her teeth and bone. My fingers press into not just skin, but muscles and joints. I push and she falls, we fall, into the bed.

The front of my shorts stands like a pyramid. Now. "Now," I say, and bump my clumsy hands against her breasts. I tear at the fabric separating her from me. I must be rid of it. But the fabric clings to her.

"It's-" Chana's breath is as rushed as mine. "It's in back," she says. "The clasp."

I grip the back panel and pull, but nothing opens. Chana throws off my hands, then reaches behind her (again with that arm-breaking contortion) and unbuckles herself. And like the dress before, the brassiere melts off her body.

Oh, her breasts are small and soft; her nipples brown and wrinkled and large in my hands, between my lips and my tongue like sweet raisins in challah. I kiss and lick every part of her, gnawing and kneading. I am on top of her, pressing myself between her legs. Chana is moaning; heat tumbles forth from her divide.

Suddenly, her hand darts down and grips me below, through the cotton of my underpants.

Never before have I been so touched, and I stop, shocked, simply feeling her fingers around me.

"Please," she says. "Now. Please." Her fingers find my elastic waistband. And they slide beneath to grip me again.

I am motionless, gape-mouthed, wordless. Her dry, warm hand travels up and down my length, burrowing into the thicket below. Her other hand tugs my underwear to my knees.

"Now," she says, withdrawing her hand to strip off her underpants as well. I grab her buttocks in my hands, crash her body against mine, kiss frantically, swipe my palms against her drenched hairiness. My greatest sensitivity is extending, extending toward hers. With a gasp, I push my sensitivity into her wetness, where all is warm and dark and plump and throbbing alive. Oh, my sensitivity is in hers and we are rocking in and out, throbbing to throbbing, crying and spilling and oh, I am buried so deep, my whole body vaults to press deeper into her heat. Then we are rubbing faster, sweat and tears and slickness pouring off us.

Chana screams and arches first, shuddering over and over and clutching my shoulders. And then the world turns red and yellow and pink and I empty into her, each pulse sweeter and sweeter and sweeter, until there is no more. No more but sweat and warmth, and Chana in my arms.

I am suddenly aware that I am still standing-slack-mouthed, vacant-eyed, wet-crotched-in Rosenbloom's Jewish Books and Religious Articles.

My eyes focus forward on a shelf of small cardboard containers. Shabbos candles, twelve to a box.

Anat. I remember: I came here to buy a present for Anat. And

I have chosen the gift I will bring to her roof, the gift I will give with desire and certainty.

I will give Anat these wax sticks and say, "When I love a woman for the first time, it will be slow, on a clean bed, with red wine, by candlelight." I will watch her eyes. And then I will walk away.

I take my candles to the Hasid behind the cash register. As he gives me my change, I notice he is careful not to touch my hand.

Knaydle and the Librarian

Elana Dykewomon

Shayna was waiting for Knaydle. The blue jeans and shirt she wore to her job as librarian at Legal Aid wouldn't do today. She dressed thoughtfully-soft salmon pink blouse, tailored brown slacks. She rubbed her hands across the pleats at the top of her thighs. These glass earrings go, she thought, holding them up to her ears in front of the mirror, the pale yellow pulling the morning's translucence into her dark face. Shayna fastened a thin gold chain to drape below the well at the base of her neck, patting her chest. Librarians, after all, are good with details.

Knaydle was round and wet but chewy. If the moon were butch she'd be Knaydle-busy trying to define the horizon, self-important, patching together fog in order to hide her sentimentality, but steady for all that, comforting. Knaydle was taking a break, renting space in the country, setting out her watercolors to find the patience to paint an acorn woodpecker. This summer she had been laid off of her night job doing newspaper paste-up and had persuaded another dyke to take over her job as coordinator of the local lesbian-save-the-world committee for seven weeks. She loved being alone in the country, where a deer might leap across the road in front of her, a fox streak out of the range of her headlights. Sometimes she knew the animals would appear before she saw them, and in those rare moments of connection she had the experience of spiritual awe-not that she ever would describe it that way when her friends asked if, perhaps, she wasn't bored during all those nights alone. Still, a few meetings in the city couldn't be avoided, and she longed for her lover as otters long for abalone. It was summer and just barely sticky in the middle of the West Coast states. Knaydle threw her laundry in the back of her pickup truck and drove the three hours into town, direct to Shayna's.

After two years, Knaydle had formed a romantic vision of her relationship with Shayna that paralleled her Hebrew school knowledge of the early kibbutz-purposeful, pleasurable days in which the desert bloomed and brought forth fruit, evenings full of thoughtful discussion, sensitive and sensual talking while they ate the pulp of warm oranges (and in that fantasy, no land had been appropriated, no one displaced for the sake of an ideal). Her ex-lovers found Knaydle's enthusiasm for the librarian hard to fathom. They saw a tall, bookish, serious, kind woman-the one who seeks the most ill-at-ease newcomer at a party to welcome in-a proper, earnest sort of woman, easy to surprise. Before Shayna, Knaydle had gone for either drama queens or adventurous rebels, dope-smoking half-burned out activists who didn't know what they wanted to do when they grew up but were worldly wise. Shayna was orderly, organized, often shy, and completely unshakable in a conversation about principles-so convinced about what was right and wrong that Knaydle's ex's thought Shayna a little, well, naive.

Finally pulling up in front of Shayna's apartment, Knaydle takes a moment of pleasure in her excellent parallel parking job. Hot from the road, she slings her bag of dirty clothes over her shoulder and cradles a dozen red roses carefully in her arm, hoping they'll catch Shayna's attention before the stains on her old T-shirt do. Knaydle moves her short, wide body through the world by force of will, trying to make her presence imply she has the right, the same right as anyone to fight for what she believes in, swim in any pool, rub her hands across a woman's skin. But under the force of will she worries and sighs: How is it possible to have ended up happy, a fat Jewish girl from Long Island?

Shayna opens the door with the intent look of a girl carefully untying a ribbon on a giant birthday present. Knaydle stares at her salmon-colored blouse (ironed, too), wishing she could raise an eyebrow, settling on bending her head forty-five degrees to angle a kiss on Shayna's cheek. Shayna grabs Knaydle's shoulder and Knaydle, drawn in, pulls away-only an hour and a half for the laundry, for reporting on everything.

"Alright, put your laundry in while I arrange the roses." Shayna says, hugging Knaydle to her breasts. "While you're downstairs, guess what I'm wearing underneath this."

Knaydle tries to imagine, positioning quarters in the washing machine slot, amazed that here in Oakland a woman would greet her this way, because after all there's that fine line between coming off as a butch or a shlub. Upstairs the roses fill Shayna's purple glass vase, made for this. "A lover," Knaydle says, struggling for composure (and breath, after bolting upstairs), "should always have a vase handy for roses."

"Just in case," Shayna agrees and then they are embracing. Knaydle opens her eyes in sensual shock and closes them as their lips fit, press, puzzle over each other, and remember the answer again. Knaydle takes Shayna's hand off her jeans and molds its palm to her cheek, surprised by desire.

"Did I make a mistake?" Shayna asks, laughing, but a little unsure underneath, her uncertainty a faint blush under her olive skin. "Aren't you my lover? Don't we do this?"

"Oh, we do." Knaydle takes a deep breath, then moves her hand to the bottom of Shayna's pants and very slowly works the top button loose, tugs the zipper slowly down-a little bit of blouse is caught, uncaught. "Maybe you're not wearing anything," Knaydle says. Then she sees the black lace-Shayna's garter belt, her stockings, the small bikini butterfly lace underwear Knaydle gave her for their first-month anniversary, laughing about how none of their friends would ever suspect.

Knaydle presses Shayna's belly with the flat of her palm, listening to her lover suck in her breath. Shayna's belly is soft and quivers. Knaydle grabs the top of the black underwear and pulls up on it sharply, so Shayna can feel the pressure, the thin line of lace taut against the ruffled outer lips, hard as it trails across her anus.

They start for the bedroom. Shayna's slacks rest open, held up by the fullness of her hips. Knaydle experiences a rush of pleasure at how well those pants fit, at the neatness of the ironed crease. Now she relaxes and expands into her own flesh, excited. She stops Shayna in the hall, pushes her up against the plaster. Shayna leans back. "Here?"

Knaydle doesn't answer. Right outside the kitchen doorway, she pulls Shayna's pants down, moving down with them, crouching on her knees. Then she reaches up to roll the underwear down Shayna's thighs to the top of her stockings where the garters are fastened. Bracing herself with one hand she can just manage to use the other to pull Shayna's outer lips open. Knaydle falls forward into that inner layering and tongues Shayna's clitoris, which swells as she slumps and tries to hold herself up against the wall.

"I know what I want for my fiftieth birthday," Shayna says.

"What?"

"This."

Pulling her, pushing her against the wall Knaydle tries out a whisper-"You're a slut." She moves back an inch to make sure Shayna heard. She watches her lover's bright green eyes disappear behind fluttering eyelids. Knaydle continues, very softly, very low, "You dress like this to make me take you. Where do you want to be taken? On the kitchen floor? In the hall? You can't wait, can you?"

"No," Shayna says, her breath catching in her throat.

Then "Yes," she says, but Knaydle can't keep it up, not the soft-core dirty talking or the licking, while crouching on her knees. She sits, but sitting she's too short to reach where Shayna's long legs deposit her sex. "My shoes," Shayna says.

Knaydle slips Shayna's feet free of the pumps, pulls Shayna's pants all the way down and off, runs her hand in a hungry sweep along the stockings from thigh to feet, the sweet slinky sensation of rub and tension crackling. She squeezes the tip of Shayna's toes but still, bunched on the floor looking up at Shayna's garter belt, can't quite reach.

"Let's go to the bed," Shayna pleads.

"Wait." Under the telephone table there's a neat stack of phone books-and luckily, Oakland is a big enough city. Knaydle puts two beneath her, making a seat.

Shayna laughs, "How come in all the lesbian sex stories it's always a perfect fit?"

"Because we don't write them," Knaydle says, now pulling Shayna back, pulling her vagina toward her mouth. Shayna's bleeding. Knaydle pushes the little tampon string out of the way. After two years, they are certain enough they have nothing dangerous, and they indulge their luck.

"I hope I don't taste like soap," Shayna worries, "having just washed."

"No, you taste clean-you taste like sex," Knaydle licks with her long strong tongue, circling, switching the membrane back and forth.

"I can't," Shayna moans. Her knees are buckling, trembling. "You're making me weak in the knees." They each suppress a giggle.

"No more clichés," Knaydle slaps Shayna's thigh lightly. "This is what you asked for, slut-you can stand it a little longer." She moves her tongue through flesh for another minute, but Shayna's right-she's starting to wilt on her feet, so Knaydle reluctantly gets up.

The bed is covered with library books and crossword puzzles, as if Shayna hadn't imagined that the seduction she'd so carefully prepared would actually work. Now she sweeps everything onto the floor and rummages through the bedside table drawer searching for the lubricant. She places the black bottle by the pillow as she lies down. Knaydle quickly pulls off her pants and shirt, leaving on a black undershirt, purple underwear.

"Who did you dress for?" Shayna laughs, grabbing for her. Knaydle sloshes beside Shayna on the water bed, unsnapping the garters so she can slip the lace underwear off. All the garters are easy except the last one, which is behind her leg. Knaydle can't see it, but finally the elastic pops back, tingles Shayna's skin.

"Sorry." Knaydle pats the back of Shayna's leg.

"It felt good," Shayna whispers.

Grinning, Knaydle finally gets the butterfly off so Shayna can spread. She takes a deep breath and exhales, feeling fat and strong beside Shayna's length. "You know how big I am, how wide you have to open to let me in," she murmurs, pulling both of Shayna's breasts from her velour sports bra while hooking one leg over Shayna's thigh. Knaydle sucks on Shayna's exposed nipples, presses against her, takes a nipple deep in her mouth, making it harden, pucker, and rise. She alternates between mouth kisses and nipple sucks as she rubs and pats Shayna's cunt. Kissing, rubbing, she closes her eyes and sees that in their flesh lie all the secrets of the Kabbalah, written in lesbian code. She wonders if later, alone, it would be possible to make a painting of the intricate patterns their bodies reveal.

"I want you sitting between my legs," Shayna says, and Knaydle forgets about the painting, rolls on her side, and shifts her weight until she's (finally) in place, caressing, rubbing, slapping Shayna's thighs, cooling her clitoris with the wet lubricant. As she sits, Knaydle pulls her tank top up, so her huge breasts rest on Shayna's legs, brushing the crease of her belly and cunt.

Shayna curves her hand around Knaydle's left breast, making a throaty sound of satisfaction.

Now Knaydle is concentrating. She gets two fingers in alongside the tampon, which surprises Shayna, who inhales sharply. Knaydle slows, looking for any sign that it might be too much, but Shayna pushes on her breast and sighs, "more, more, more." Knaydle rubs her cunt with two fingers, while pushing in with the other hand. The tension strains her back and she shifts, wishing for a wall to lean against, uncomfortable struggling for position against the undulating surface of the bed-the only hitch in this, but not anything that she'd let stop her.

Talking helps her focus on Shayna. "Take more-you know you've been wanting this. Everyone thinks you're so proper, so refined, but I know better. You're not just my girl-" Knaydle stops breathing for a second, overwhelmed by the bright gray sensation of doing this, saying these words, then exhales, slightly dizzy, intent "-you're my slut, and the more you want, the more I'm going to make you take. I'm not going to stop, not going to let up. You have to take more-c'mon, I want to see you take it. Take more." Shayna groans and writhes, arches, widens, and then her legs tighten.

Pulling her fingers out, Knaydle holds Shayna's cunt open with one hand, keeps rubbing Shayna's clit with two fingers of the other. Shayna stays tight and Knaydle feels a film cover her face, her eyes-now she has the sensation that a deer will materialize beside them, as she had two days ago driving on route 20 just before a deer ran across the slope above the road, and as she stares into her image of the deer's face, her lover comes.

Shayna pulls her whole body up-the muscles clamp spasm

clamp she sits up her mouth opens but only a small oh escapes and then a longer one she leans back rises again oh oh all the gush of wind in the body, wind and liquid running, pushing at the boundaries. Knaydle is laughing, pleased with herself, maneuvering back at last to lie against Shayna's side. A little fussy, she reaches for a tissue to wipe the juice and blood and lubricant goo off her hand before wrapping an arm around her lover.

Often Shayna falls asleep after she comes, but this time she says, "I'm too excited and I don't want to miss a minute of you." Shayna runs her palm across the arc of Knaydle's belly, then slips her fingers under the lowest fold and rocks her flesh. Knaydle shudders, but she can't keep from remembering what time it is.

"Honey, I can't, I have to go to the meeting-"

Shayna shakes her head, pulls Knaydle's hand to her mouth, kissing it. "And everyone thinks I'm the one who's controlled."

"I'm not controlled-just on a schedule. I've only got thirty minutes, and I have to change. Don't worry, I'll be back."

"Worried, I'm not," Shayna says, almost to herself. She changes into her jeans and the T-shirt from the Italian restaurant around the corner that says "Escape Responsibility" on the back, while Knaydle puts her clothes in the dryer downstairs.

Shayna warms up leftover tofu and rice. She realizes she's smiling at her rice and puts down her fork, watching Knaydle finish.

"Who would know," Knaydle says, wiping her mouth, getting up to leave, "to look at you-such a nice Jewish lady, a librarian, even-what a slut you really are."

"Don't tell," Shayna says.

"No one?"

"No one."

"How about if I write a story about it?"

"That would be okay."

"It's okay to tell everyone but not to tell anyone?"

"Exactly," Shayna says, blushing, and Knaydle pulls Shayna's hands to the curve of her cheek again, taking the time, breathless, on her way.

Love Ruins Everything

Karen X. Tulchinsky

The last rays of the setting sun reflect off the Castro Theater marquee, shining brilliantly through the window onto the table at our favorite Thai restaurant in San Francisco. We come here every Tuesday night for their special on seafood curry. I squint at my lover through the glare. Sapphire smiles, reaches for her glass of white wine.

"I think we should become nonmonogamous," she announces, taking a sip.

"*What?*" A chunk of curried prawn lodges in my throat.

Sapphire sets her wineglass down. Sucks in a deep breath. "I've wanted to talk to you about this all day."

I swallow hard, try to force the prawn down. "You have?"

"I've been thinking about it."

"Since when?"

She picks up her fork, plays with a piece of sautéed eggplant. "Since yesterday."

"Yesterday? What happened yesterday? I thought you went for groceries."

"I did."

"At Safeway."

"I did."

"And then you came home."

"Right." She stabs mercilessly at the eggplant. At the next table, a mere three inches away, a forty-something gay white couple are talking about a new software program that will revolutionize the banking industry. Both have short gray hair, balding on top. One has a mustache, the other a goatee. Their sweaters are in matching chartreuse.

"And while you were shopping you decided we should be nonmonogamous?"

"Yes. No. Well…not while I was shopping. I don't know when. I just did."

I fold my arms across my chest. "Who is she?" I blurt, a little on the loud side.

"Nomi." Sapphire glances nervously at the sweater fags. There's a lull in their scintillating conversation. Forks scrape against plates. "Lower your voice."

"Why?" I shout. "I've got nothing to hide." Sapphire hates "a scene in public." Her WASP upbringing is deeply ingrained.

"Nomi, I won't discuss this if you keep shouting." Someone's cell phone rings.

"Who's shouting?" I yell. The fags raise their eyebrows in our direction.

"Hello?" A man behind me answers his phone.

Sapphire tosses her napkin on the table and stands. "I'm leaving," she whispers, glancing furtively about the room. Everyone around us is listening, half-hoping she'll throw wine in my face or slap me. Better story for their friends.

"Sapphire." I whine. "Come on. Sit down. You haven't finished yet." She shakes her head, silently fumes across the restaurant and out the door. I signal for the waiter. An instrumental version of "Have You Ever Loved a Woman?" is playing softly in the background.

I pay and run up the hill to our flat on States Street, the home I've shared with Sapphire for two and a half years. Jody, Sapphire's gray tabby, and The Twins—Martina and Whitney, two all-black kittens she recently brought home from the animal shelter—scamper over. Sapphire is lying on the couch in a knee-length Gay Freedom Day 1993 T-shirt, watching *The Simpsons*. I stand beside the TV and watch her.

"Are you going to sit down?" She's still angry.

It occurs to me that I should be the angry one. "Are you going to talk to me? No one can hear us now," I say icily. It drives me crazy that she's so uptight. My family screams and carries on in public all the time. It's as natural as breathing.

Sapphire shuts off the television and makes room for me on the sofa. I sit cross-legged, facing her. She takes my hands and gazes at me with a sweet, loving expression, the very look I fell in love with in the first place. "I don't want to hurt your feelings, Nomi. I love you. It's just that…I've always gone right from one relationship to the next, with no space in between. I've never really been single, and I don't know how to date."

"It's not all it's cracked up to be."

She sighs. "Maybe so, but I need to find out for myself. I don't want to break up with you to do it. I just want to try my hand at dating. Can you understand that?"

"Sure, I understand. You're bored with me and you're looking for someone new." I sulk, turning away from her.

She leans forward to gaze into my eyes. "Nomi. I'm not bored with you."

I face her. "If you dump me for someone else I'll kill you."

She touches my cheek tenderly. "I'm not dumping you."

"I'll shoot you. I don't care if I spend the rest of my life in jail. I'll do it."

"Come here." Her hands draw me to her for a kiss.

The next day, I'm strolling down Castro, on a warm, sunny early November afternoon. The morning fog has lifted, revealing a pure blue sky. I'm carrying a bag of groceries, a box of croissants, and cut flowers for Sapphire, all of which slip from my grasp and slide to the dirty sidewalk when a huge muscular man with a buzz cut, baggy pants, and a baseball cap bends forward and French kisses my girlfriend. I stare at them. Everyone else stares at me.

"Hey lady," an adolescent boy shouts. "You dropped your stuff."

The lovebirds break apart. Sapphire's eyes are soft and dreamy. She enjoyed being mauled by this Rambo. I stand, transfixed. The guy shifts to one side and Sapphire's eyes connect with mine. She freezes, like a kid caught smoking cigarettes or stealing candy. I glare pure contempt at her. She rushes toward me. Every muscle in my body flinches and I turn away, leaving everything on the ground.

"Nomi," she yells. "Stop!"

I stomp up the street.

"Nomi! Wait! Let's talk about this."

"What's to say?" I yell over my shoulder. It's uphill and I start to breathe heavily.

"Nomi. What about your stuff? You can't just leave it here."

"The hell I can't."

Then I don't feel her behind me anymore. She's stopped to pick up the groceries. I march right past our street and keep walking. And walking.

"I knew it," my mother says, when I call her in Toronto later that evening. Sapphire is out. We had a huge fight when I finally came home. She bolted, slamming the door behind her. I'm sipping a glass of Sapphire's fifteen-year-old port. A present from her father she's never opened.

"What? What did you know, Ma?"

"I knew she wasn't a real lesbian." There is smug satisfaction in my mother's voice, like she's just solved the bonus phrase on *Wheel of Fortune*.

"Ma. What do you mean, a 'real lesbian'?"

"I always thought she was very feminine."

"Yeah? She was—is. So?"

"So? So, she probably really likes men."

"Ma, that makes no sense. Feminine doesn't have anything to do with it. Anyway, since when are you such an expert on lesbians?"

"I learned everything I know from you and a little from Phil Donahue too. Did you see the show about lesbian serial killers?"

"Ma, don't start with me. Please. Are you listening? Me and Sapphire are breaking up. It's just like a divorce, Ma. I'm a wreck. I want sympathy. I don't want Phil Donahue."

Silence. I can picture my mother nodding her head. I glance at the photo taken last December on our second anniversary, framed on Sapphire's fake-oak entertainment centre. We look happy and in love. I flip it facedown. Hard. Unfortunately, the glass doesn't break. "You're right, Nomi. What was I thinking? I'm sorry. Can you forgive me? How are you, dear? You need anything? Why don't you come home? You can stay with me. It'll be fun. We'll have pyjama parties."

"Ma, I'm too old for pyjama parties and so are you."

"You're never too old for a little fun. Remember that, *mamelah*. It's very important."

"I'm staying here."

"What's to stay for? Why don't you come home?"

"This is my home, Ma. I live here now."

"Okay. You can't blame me for trying. So? Tell me. Are you okay for money? I'll send a little something to help out."

My mother the millionaire. We weren't exactly the Rockefellers when my father was alive. Now, she gets by on a small pension from an insurance policy my father left her, and part-time work in the synagogue gift shop. "Since when are you so flush? What? Did somebody die?"

"Nobody died. It's Murray."

"What? He gives you money?" Murray Feinstein is the man my mother has been dating. They met a year ago at the cemetery, after my father's unveiling. Murray was at the cemetery that day, paying respects to his wife.

"Watch your mouth, young lady. I'm still your mother."

"What did I say?"

189

"He takes me out three, four times a week for dinner, Chinese, Italian, steak, you name it. So, my grocery bill is a little lower these days."

"Oh."

I pretend to be asleep when Sapphire leaves for work the next morning. We work completely different hours. I tend bar Thursday to Sunday evenings at Patty's Place, a small neighborhood pub in Bernal Heights. Sapphire's on day shift, Monday to Friday, at Good Vibrations, the sex toy shop in the Mission, which is hilarious. If her customers knew how uptight and repressed she really is, she'd never sell a single dildo. At the kitchen table, I sit with a cold cup of coffee for hours, in a state of shock. Sapphire lived in this apartment with her last lover, too. This is Sapphire's apartment. Apart from that one picture of us, all the photos are of Sapphire's family. Her grandparents, Nanna and Poppa, her parents, her two blond brothers and her thin sister. All smiling. No one touches. The furniture, dishes, stereo, TV, the books, towels, knickknacks are Sapphire's. I have my clothes, a couple of books, comb, toothbrush, gel, my helmet. Once we bought a garlic press together—hers was rusty. And the bed. We both chipped in for a new bed. The rest is all Sapphire's.

When I finally check the clock, the whole day has gone. It's time to get ready for work. Sapphire will be asleep when I come home later. I feel like the earth has tilted and I'm slowly sliding into a big, empty pit. I don't know what to do.

Tonight Sapphire wants to have dinner with me. I haven't

seen her all weekend. She was out when I was home. Or sleeping. I was at work while she was here. She saunters in the door glowing, like someone newly in love.

"Hi, Nomi," she says, all casual, and slips past me into the bedroom. She's an hour late. I fume at the kitchen table. I bet she squeezed in a visit with Rambo. A silent rage bubbles up from the pit of my belly.

"I'm going to grab a quick shower," she chirps from the bedroom, "then we can go out."

I march into our room, fists clenched at my sides. "No, Sapphire. We can't." I say to the back of her head.

She swivels around. "What?"

"You're an hour late."

"Am I?" She glances at the nonexistent watch on her naked arm.

"Look, I'm not a fool," I say, although it's not exactly true.

"Nomi..." She takes a step toward me.

"You were with *him*, weren't you?"

She sighs.

"That's what I thought." I go to the closet, yank open the door, search through a pile of laundry for my black canvas knapsack. Angrily, I heave dirty clothes behind me into the room.

"Nomi, what are you doing?"

"Shit." Frustrated, I grab a tennis racket and toss it clattering onto the hardwood floor. An old bottle of sunscreen, a baseball, broken sunglasses, a running shoe, white extension cord, I hurl them all. "There." I haul out my canvas bag, cram in a few pairs of underwear, jeans, a couple of T-shirts, socks, push past Sapphire into the bathroom. My toothbrush, our toothpaste, my comb, cologne, and face soap I stuff into the front pouch.

"Nomi. What are you doing?"

"Sapphire, I think the question is, what are *you* doing?" I fling the knapsack onto my back, wrench the front door open so violently it bangs against the wall, and race down the stairs to the street. Fog obliterates the sun, casting a pall over the earth.

I roar down States Street on my red Honda Rebel. On Castro I pull over to the curb. Where will I go? The whole week has been nothing but pain. Every moment in that apartment with Sapphire is salt on an open wound. At 18th, I make a sudden U-turn and stop at the pay phone in front of A Different Light Bookstore, where I call Betty, my best friend.

"Get over here, girl," she orders. Betty lives alone in a one-bedroom apartment in Bernal Heights, not far from where I work. "Living room couch is all yours, babe," Betty says, "for as long as you want. You hear?"

"You're a lifesaver, Betty."

"You can flatter me later. Just get your white butt over here."

I jump back on my bike and ride up the Castro Street hill. Cool wind blows against my hot face. I'm so angry my emotional tremors could trigger a small earthquake.

"It's Sapphire again." Betty pokes her freshly shaved head through the bedroom doorway, holding the phone receiver. "What do you want me to tell her?"

"Tell her to go to hell!"

Betty speaks into the phone. "Did you hear that? Uh-huh. Okay. Yep. I'll tell her." She passes through the living room to the kitchen, returns with two cans of Bud Light, and hands me one. I screw up my face but accept the beer and swallow a big swig. "How can you drink this stuff? It's terrible."

"You don't seem to mind." Betty sits beside me on the couch. Out of habit, she brushes the air behind her ear where her dreadlocks used to be, then leans back against oversized, multi-colored pillows. Betty'd had dreads since 1985. Yesterday, she cut them off, shaved her head right down to the scalp. Says she's been cold ever since. "Want to know what she said?" Betty pulls the quilt from the end of the couch up over her legs. With the remote control, she switches on her thirty-inch TV screen. Stereo sound emanates from the speakers. She flips through the channels, stops at *The Simpsons*..

"I hate this show," I announce, bitchily.

She looks at me like I've lost my mind. "You love this show."

I shrug. "I hate it. So? What did she say?"

She hesitates, examines my face.

"What?" I say, unnerved by her stare.

"You're not going to like it."

"So? What else is new? Tell me what she said."

"She says she never meant to hurt you. She never meant to...you sure you want to hear it?"

I beat my fist on the armrest. "I said I did. Just tell me."

"Okay. She says she never meant tofallinlovewithRichard. It just happened." Betty spits the words like she can't wait to get them out of her mouth.

This is too much for me. I leap up off the couch. A stream of beer shoots from the top of my can onto Betty. "Richard? Richard! Just happened? Oh, great! That's just great. It just happened," I repeat, as sarcastically as humanly possible. "How fucking original. Isn't that fucking original, Betty?"

"Not particularly." She dumps the beer-soaked quilt to the floor, raises her butt, reaches into her back pocket, extracts a blue bandanna, and mops beer from her face and chest. Her black sweatshirt soaks up the rest of it.

"I can't believe this." I sink onto the couch, slam my beer can down on the end table, drop my face into my hands, and begin to cry. Betty leans over, rubs my back, and drinks her beer.

"Oh god," I let the tears flow.

"Poor Nomi."

"Oh shit. I can't do this. I can't cry."

"It's okay, Nomi. I won't tell anyone."

"No. It's not that. I have to work tonight."

"Oh."

I lift my head. "My eyes are all red and puffy already. Aren't they?"

She leans back to take a real good look at me. "Well...not so bad."

"You're lying."

She shrugs.

"Shit. I gotta stop crying." I say, which unleashes a new torrent. Betty makes sympathetic noises, strokes my back.

"Why don't you call in sick?"

"Patty'll kill me."

"No she won't. She'll understand. In fact, I think you should take the whole week off. You can't work in this condition." Betty reaches for the phone, hands me the receiver. "Go ahead. Call her."

"You think?" I sniff.

Betty nods.

I dial the number. The dog in the next apartment begins to bark.

On Betty's living room sofa, I toss and turn all night. It's an ancient loveseat that does not pull out into a bed. Even at five-two, I am too long. If I lie on my back and stretch my legs out, I have to perch them on the opposite armrest. On my side in the fetal position, my knees bang against the back. Before sunup, the woman in the next apartment is awake, clattering dishes into cupboards. A pillow over my head does not muffle the clanging of pots. Later, Betty bounds in, wearing long johns under her jeans and a sweatshirt, even though bright sun streams through the living room window. "I'm going to Cafe Blue for a cappuccino," she says. "Wanna come?"

I drag the covers over my head. The quilt smells like stale beer. "No! I'm never going there again. Me and Sapphire used to go every Sunday morning."

"Well, it's Saturday."

Betty saves us a table on the patio. I go inside for drinks. Balancing two cappuccinos in one hand, a gigantic piece of chocolate cake in the other, and a recent copy of the *Bay Times* under my arm, I squeeze my way through the narrow, crowded café. Almost at our table, I try to push past an unusually tall man. When I look up I'm face to face with Sapphire. The tall guy is him. Rambo. For a brief second I consider throwing hot coffee in Sapphire's face. She sees what I'm thinking. Her eyes widen, she looks at the cups, then back at me.

"Don't you just wish I was that immature?" I spit.

She extends her hands out in front of her. "Nomi. Please. Can't we just talk?"

"About what?" I thrust everything into her open arms. I don't look back when something crashes to the floor. Betty follows me outside.

"Okay. So coffee was a bad idea. But you know what I would do?" Betty sits on the living room floor, trying to decipher the instructions for her new CD player. She's nagging me to go out. All I do is mope around her apartment. I can tell I'm getting on her nerves.

"What?" I push a pile of silver paper clips to one side of the coffee table and a pile of brass ones to the other side. I've taken to sorting through Betty's junk drawers. It settles my nerves to put something in order, even if it isn't my life.

"Go out. Get laid. Have fun. Believe me, there's nothing better for heartbreak than sex. Nothing." She waves the CD player instruction booklet at me.

"What's this?" I show her a small metal object that might have once been a plastic key chain, covered in bubble gum so old it's melted. Underneath is a faint illustration of the Golden Gate Bridge.

Betty lunges forward, grabs the chain, and hurls it into the garbage can. I decide to go out soon, if only to make Betty happy.

Later that night, Betty has a date. I rent *Moonstruck*, the only movie I can stand to watch. I open a can of Bud Light, pull Betty's quilt over my legs and settle in for the evening. During my second beer, my favorite scene begins. Late night in New York City. Loretta Casterini and Ronny Cammerari stand outside Ronny's apartment building. A cold winter evening; light snow falls as the new lovers argue.

"Love isn't perfeck," Ronny declares. "Love breaks your heart. Love ruins everything."

I know the scene word for word. I speak the lines with Ronny, imitating a thick New York accent, and just like him, I pronounce "perfect" "perfeck."

"We're not here to make things perfeck. The snowflakes are perfeck. The stars are perfeck. Not us. Not us. We are here to ruin ourselves and to break our hearts and love the wrong people, and—and die."

A single tear rolls down my cheek. I never thought our relationship was perfeck, but I thought we had a good thing. I miss Sapphire, even though I hate her. As I drift off to sleep the titles roll and Dean Martin sings,

"When the moon hits your eye like a big pizza pie, that's amore.

When you dance down the street, with a cloud at your feet, you're in love.

When you walk in a dream

But you know you're not dreaming, Signora.

'Scuza me, but you see

Back in old Napoli, that's amore."

I dream I'm in an old four-poster bed. Around me are scantily dressed women whose sole purpose in life is to make me happy. One is kissing me. Another rubs my feet. Someone fixes me a drink. Someone else pays my rent. It's a lovely dream with a multimillion-dollar budget and a cast of thousands, all of them beautiful. Sapphire roams in, wearing a black negligee, slips into bed beside me, pours tiny kisses all over my body. It's just like old times. We kiss. She touches me everywhere with silk fingers. I feel a peace I'd almost forgotten about.

I wake to keys jingling in the lock. Giggling. Betty and some woman I don't recognize creep into the apartment, trying unsuccessfully, in their intoxicated state, to be quiet.

"It's okay," I announce, "I'm not sleeping."

Silence. Then, "Hi, Nomi. Sorry to wake you."

"I wasn't sleeping." I drag the covers over my head as they make their way to Betty's room, one paper-thin wall over. I try not to listen while they have sex. With my head under the covers I'm in a cave. It's pitch black. My heart hurts, beating cruelly against the inside of my chest. Quietly, with resignation, I cry. How did my life fall apart so quickly? Sleep creeps over the muffled sounds of Betty and her friend.

The next morning I decide to take Betty's advice. I ask for her help getting back into circulation. Betty knows everyone. She fixes me up with Alison, the younger sister of a woman Betty dated last year.

"Oh. Did I mention she just came out recently?" Betty asks as I'm about to leave.

"What?"

"She's a little shy," says Betty.

Alison and I go to the Castro Theater. They're showing Forrest Gump. I missed it when it first came out. Halfway through the film I casually slip my hand into Alison's. It's nice to touch someone again, but I'm acutely aware that the hand is not Sapphire's. It's thinner, the grip is weaker. Tears roll down my cheeks as the movie ends. I pretend they're for Forrest, but really, they're for me. And Sapphire. I fake a smile and suggest a drink at The Cafe, a second-story bar overlooking Market.

At the door, Alison is asked for ID. Suddenly, I feel old. My whole life seems ridiculous. Why did I listen to Betty? I don't want to date. I want Sapphire.

"Alison, maybe we should just..."

The bouncer gives back her ID and nods okay. She smiles.

"What were you saying?"

"Nothing." We wander over to stools at an empty table by the window. The radio towers of Twin Peaks loom over the Castro.

Alison and I don't have much to say to each other. I'm new at dating, and she's new, period. I scramble for small talk. The movie, the weather, our jobs, the community. After two drinks I'm enjoying myself. Maybe Betty's right. Maybe an affair would lift my spirits. I look at Alison. She is attractive. I smile. She smiles. The DJ slides on "Mighty Good Man" by Salt and Pepa and En Vogue.

"Wanna dance?" I ask.

She smiles again. I lead her to the dance floor. I watch her hips sway from side to side as we dance. Her breasts are round and full in low-cut spandex. She looks more inviting by the moment. I wrap an arm around her waist. We dance tightly together, her body against mine. She feels different from Sapphire. Smaller around, a little taller, and she moves more slowly. She looks deep into my eyes, licks her lips. I think she wants me to kiss her. I lean forward, slowly bring my lips to hers. She presses her mouth against mine hard. Her tongue searches inside my mouth, soft breasts against mine, fingers in my hair. Rum and coke on her tongue. We kiss until the song ends. She grins.

"Maybe we should go somewhere...more comfortable," I whisper in her ear.

"Mmmm," she says in response.

We ride up Divisadero on my Honda and park on the sidewalk outside Alison's small ground-floor studio apartment on Haight. Her barred windows are covered in grime. Cars rush by, people yell, buses roar, music blares, panhandlers beg, dogs bark. The apartment reeks of cat piss. Footsteps pound overhead. The floor is sticky. Four hundred dishes crowd the sink.

"Oh, damn," Alison curses, rushes over to the bed and feels the sheets. "Not again."

"What?"

"My cat's neurotic. Whenever I'm out, she pees on the bed."

"Oh." I laugh, even though it isn't particularly funny. "Come here."

She doesn't.

"What?" I ask gently.

"Uh," she puts her head down, "it's just that…uh…"

"What?"

She looks into my eyes, hers dreamy with lust. "Kiss me."

I do. We kiss for a long time. We grope each other through our clothes. My nipples are hard. I'm getting wet. Desire pounds against the stone fortress that surrounded my heart and seized my body the day I saw Sapphire kissing that guy on Castro. I ease Alison's corduroy jacket off her shoulders, toss it away. I undo the first small button on her sweater, the second button and the third. Her body stiffens slightly. Her hand grasps my wrist.

"What? What's wrong?"

She looks down again.

"Alison?"

"Look. Maybe you'd better go."

"Go? But I thought you said…"

"I did, but I'm…just not ready."

"Not ready?"

"You know."

"Oh." I drop my hands to my sides. "Oh." I say again. "Are you okay?" I try to see her eyes, but they're hidden behind her long, straight hair. Maybe she's crying. "Well, okay. I'll go then. Uh, if that's what you want. That is what you want, right? For me to go?" I want to part her hair so I can see her eyes, but I'm afraid to touch her. She nods. "Well…ah…I'll…I'll call you. Okay?" I open the door quietly and let myself out.

"Don't be ridiculous, Ma. Of course I know about safe sex." I sip steaming coffee, reclining against the large pillow on Betty's couch.

"All right. I was only asking. Just in case, I picked up a few pamphlets at my doctor's office."

"Don't send pamphlets. I know what they say." Betty meanders into the room, naked from the waist up. She's growing more used to having no hair and has stopped dressing for the North Pole. She passes the couch, heads for the kitchen, rubbing her eyes, stretching. Her baggy, navy blue Joe Boxers go all the way down to her knees. Sunlight floods the living room.

"It's no trouble, Nomi. A fifty-two-cent stamp I can afford."

"Please, Ma. Keep the pamphlets. Okay?" I hear Betty pour herself a cup of coffee.

"What can I say? A mother worries."

"Don't worry, I know all about it. Anyway, lesbians are a low-risk group." Betty trudges in with her coffee and sinks down beside me on the couch.

"*Mamelah*, what are you talking about—'low-risk'?"

"Ma. It's hard to explain." Betty raises her eyebrows and smiles broadly.

"I'm listening."

"The AIDS virus is…" I grope for words. "More present in sperm and blood than…anywhere else."

Silence. Betty puts her ear up to the receiver to listen in.

"Ma?"

"I'm listening. Go on."

I look to Betty for help.

A week later B.J., Betty's girlfriend-of-the-week, introduces me to her friend Mimi, a librarian, a few years older than me, also recently divorced. She still lives with her ex. I don't know how she does it. I can barely stand the thought of Sapphire, never mind the sight of her. I ask Mimi out.

A steep flight of wooden stairs leads to a pale green Victorian with large bay windows, a fake front, and ornamental trim circling white stone pillars. No one answers the bell. A TV blares the theme song from Ellen out an open window on the second floor. I ring again. I knock. I ring until I hear footsteps, nervously run a hand through my short hair to smooth it down. The door opens. Mimi is wearing a silk burgundy dressing gown over bare legs. Long brown hair tied back in a braid. Soft, brown eyes.

I smile. "Hi."

"Oh, I guess you didn't get my message."

"Message?"

"I called to cancel. I'm tired. Had a rough day."

"Oh."

"Well…"

"Uh, well, would you like to take a rain check? We could go out some other time."

"Sure. Ah…what the heck. As long as you're here, we could go down the street for a coffee."

"Okay."

"But wait. I've got to get dressed." She shuts the door, leaving me on the front stoop. I lean back against the wall and watch people walk by.

Twenty minutes later the door opens. Mimi is wearing tight black jeans, a red V-neck sweater, black leather jacket. Her hair hangs halfway down her back. I hold out my arm for her as we stroll down the street.

We talk over double lattes. Her life sounds even crazier than mine. She's spent four years with a big old butch called Nat, formerly Teresa Maria. They haven't had sex in over three years.

"But the first six months were great," Mimi stresses.

She still calls Nat "her partner" even though they broke up nine months ago, when Nat announced she was a "female to male transsexual" and entered the sex-change program at the University of California, San Francisco.

For the last six months, Mimi has been dating a bisexual woman named Wanda, who also isn't having sex with her.

"I go to her place and we watch videos. I come on to her and she says she's tired," says Mimi. "Every single time. I don't know what to do."

I haven't a stitch of advice to give. "More coffee?"

We're having a good time, so we go for steak-and-whole-bean burritos at the Taqueria on 18th, and then she wants to go home.

"I'll walk you," I offer.

On the porch at her place, I wait while she opens the door. She smiles, reaches over and brushes hair out of my eyes. "Would you like to come in for a bit?"

"What about Nat?"

"Gone to visit her mother in Sacramento. She's going to tell her tonight."

"Tell her what?"

"About her sex-change operation." She takes my hand. Hers is soft and warm. I squeeze gently. She leads me up a steep flight of stairs and into a large two-bedroom flat with ten-foot-high ceilings. In the living room an ornate crystal chandelier hangs from a ceiling trimmed in swirls of plaster. A large fireplace with a hand-carved baroque mantle dominates one whole wall. The polished hardwood is covered with a red-flowered throw rug. Built-in glass cabinets are crammed full of video cassettes, CDs, and books. We sip bottles of Corona on a beige couch, its wide seat built for long-legged people. I sit forward to compensate.

"So?" Mimi says.

"So."

She sips her beer.

I sip mine. The glass bottle cools my sweaty palms.

"How long did you say you and Sapphire were together?"

"I didn't." I stare into her eyes. She smiles. I move closer.

"Oh." Again she lifts her beer bottle to her mouth, tips it back.

"Three years. Well, it would have been three years next month. Hah. I was going to take her to the Russian River for our

anniversary. Anyway, who cares? You have really beautiful eyes."
The last person I feel like talking about right now is Sapphire.

She bats them. "I do?"

"Yeah." I grin.

"Thanks."

"I'd like to kiss you," I risk.

Mimi looks nervous, but shrugs and says, "Okay."

I shift sideways, position my lips against hers. I kiss her, but she just sits there, not kissing back. I retreat.

"Don't you want me to?"

"I thought I did," she sighs. Bites her lower lip with her front teeth. "You're very attractive." She plays with my hair. "It's just that I realize I'm still in love with Nat. It feels wrong to kiss someone else."

"I thought you said you broke up?"

"We did."

"And she's a transsexual now, or whatever you call it."

"FTM."

"So how can you be in love with her?"

"I don't know. I just am."

"Well, Mimi." I grope for something to say. "Well. As a friend—that is, if I was your friend—I'd say you're selling yourself short. I mean, you said you haven't had sex with her for three years, and the bisexual isn't having sex with you either."

"Yeah? So? What's your point?"

"Uh," I laugh, unnerved by her building anger. "Well, nothing I guess. I guess I have no point."

"'Cause you don't know anything about it."

"No," I agree.

"It's complicated."

"Yeah?"

"Yeah." She crosses her arms over her breasts.

"Yeah. I mean, yeah, I see what you mean." I stall, trying desperately to coax her back to her former pleasant mood.

She yawns. Suddenly and dramatically. Deposits her beer bottle on the coffee table.

I wait.

She yawns again. I take the hint.

"Well. I guess I should be going." I place my bottle on the table beside hers and stand, hoping she'll grab my arm, say she's sorry, beg me to stay. She remains silent as I slip on my jacket. "Well," I stick out my hand.

She shakes it lamely.

"Good-bye." I let myself out.

"Who says I'm depressed?" I'm sitting cross-legged on Betty's couch with the quilt over my head, like a tent. Talking to my mother.

"Believe me, Nomi. A mother knows."

"Ma, that is so cliché." I raise the quilt up at the bottom to let in some air.

"Are you eating?"

"Yeah, Ma. Last night I ate a whole box of Oreos."

"You didn't."

"Okay. Half a box."

Betty struggles to sew a button onto a black denim shirt. I've never seen a worse attempt. Jabbing her finger, losing the needle, sewing the shirt closed by accident.

"Give me that." I snatch it and start stitching properly.

"Why don't you come, too? We're going dancing at The Wet Spot. It'll be fun. Maybe you'll meet someone."

"No thanks. I'm through with dating. I'm no good at it." I twist the end of the thread into a knot and break it with my teeth.

Betty laughs. "Girl, you'll be fine. You just need more practice. Come on. I'll wait while you get ready."

I check the rest of the buttons on her shirt. "No. I'm going to stay in and watch *Moonstruck*."

"Again?"

I fling the shirt at Betty. She catches it in midair.

Betty showers, tries on several outfits, shines her shoes, reorganizes her wallet, clips the chain to her belt loop, reshaves her head, exchanges the silver stud in her pierced lip for a gold ring. When she finally leaves, I slip *Moonstruck* into the VCR and settle down on the couch with a bowl of popcorn, a bottle of Dr Pepper, and Betty's quilt. Dean Martin begins to croon. The telephone rings.

"Hello?"

Silence.

"Hello? Hello? Who's there?"

"It's me," Sapphire says quietly.

Silence.

"Hello? Nomi?"

"Yeah. I'm still here. What do you want?"

Silence.

"I want to see you. Can I come over?"

"No."

"Nomi, please? I want to talk to you."

"Why?" My heart pounds. Sapphire's voice moves me more than I want it to. I put a hand on my rib cage.

"Can't I come over to Betty's? I want to talk in person."

"What happened? Did he dump you?"

Silence.

I laugh cruelly. "He did, didn't he?"

"Yes." Quietly.

Silence.

"What do you want me to do about it?"

"I want to talk. I'm coming over."

"No! Don't bother." I hang up. Loudly.

Ten minutes later the doorbell rings. I open the door. Sapphire's been crying. I want to tell her to go to hell, but I can't. She looks crushed. I hold the door open wide. She slips out of her shoes and plods past me. I follow. In the middle of the living room, hands at her sides, she gazes at me, her eyes soft, full of emotion. It might be love. It could also be regret, or guilt.

"I made a mistake. Nomi. I don't know what else to say. It's over now. Please. I want you back."

I slump down on the couch, snatch up my bowl of popcorn, and balance it in my lap. "Are you crazy?"

Sapphire sits beside me. "Maybe I am. I don't know. I miss you."

I shove a handful of popcorn in my mouth and chew loudly. On the TV, Loretta Casterini is fixing Ronny Cammerari a steak.

"Nomi…" Sapphire lays a hand on my arm. Her familiar touch soothes and infuriates me at the same time. I turn to look at her. She's crying. "I'm sorry, Nomi. I love you."

My head feels like a helium balloon straining to float away. I don't know what to do. This has never happened to me before. I leap up, plunk the popcorn onto the end table, and pace back and forth on the living room carpet.

"Let me get this straight, Sapphire. You met some guy, fell in love, got dumped, and now you want me back?"

She nods her head and sighs.

I laugh bitterly, shake my head. "That's great, Sapphire. That is truly twisted. How do you think I've felt these last three weeks? What do you think this has been like for me? You think I can just forget that you dumped our three-year relationship on account of some *guy*? Some *straight* guy?"

"He's bi."

"Oh great. Even better. I hope you used condoms."

"I know you're mad…"

"Mad? Mad? Are you kidding? I'm furious. And hurt. And humiliated…and lonely."

"Me too," she says. "I miss you."

I turn my back to her and face the television. With one drastic swing of his good arm, Ronny Cammerari sweeps the dinner dishes, table and all, onto the kitchen floor. He crosses the room, embraces Loretta, and they kiss. The music swells to a crescendo. I face Sapphire. I know her so well. Everything about her.

"You didn't miss me so much last week. Did you?"

"Nomi. Please, don't do this." Sapphire's head follows me like a spectator at a tennis match. I pace again.

"So? Was the sex good?"

"Nomi…"

I step closer, so I tower over her. "Was it?"

She bounds up and stands at the window, her back to me. Sounds drift up from the street. Two men laughing and talking.

"Was it?" I scream at Sapphire.

She pivots around and glares at me. Sighs. "Want do you want, Nomi?"

"Answer my question. Was it good?"

"It was…" she frowns, looks off to the side.

"What?"

"Different. It was different. Okay? That's all. Just different."

I stare at Sapphire. Different. Is that what she was looking for? Something different? She stares back. Frowns. Like she's trying to guess what I'm thinking. And then my body betrays me. I want her. I want to touch her. I hate her and want her at the same time. I imagine what it would be like to just reach over and take her in my arms. It would feel so regular. Like something I do every day. Not weird at all.

Outside, there is a terrible screech of car brakes, the unmistakable crunch of metal on metal, a cacophony of horns. A woman screams. I stare at Sapphire, my eyes set, determined. Wordless, I cross the room. She gasps. Her hand flies to her forehead as if she were a Southern belle, dazed from the heat and too much gin.

Outside, a man is yelling. A car alarm sounds.

I seize Sapphire by the shoulders, crush my lips on hers, frantic. She moans, kisses me back, flings her arms around my neck. Like Ronny Cammerari, I bend down and sweep her up. Carry her to the couch.

"Nomi?"

"Shhh."

I am lost in the sweet familiarity of her body against mine. My desire is reckless, rash. Hands on her face, I devour her lips. Her tongue in my mouth carries me back to our home together, our life. Our first time and all the other times in one climactic moment. I lunge for her breasts. She tears at my shirt. Naked, wild, desperate, flying on angel-hair wings, to the skies, to the sea, to the beautiful sea,

"You and me, you and me, oh how happy we'd be.

When the moon hits your eye, like a big pizza pie, that's amore.

When the world sees a shine, like you've had too much wine, you're in love."

My fingers are inside her. I know her so well. Know just how she likes it. She moves circles on me, pushing and sliding. Soft and wet. My face in her breasts. Warm, slippery, red fire. Tight waves crash and break. We kiss. She moans. I feel her inside me. Searching, hungry, reaching for my center, my heart. Oh honey, oh baby, I miss you. I want you.

"Yes, baby, yes!"

Her hair in my face, sweet scent of her, on my tongue, my fingers, my mouth. She bites my nipples. Raw, sweet pleasure. Sliding in and out of her, of me, of my life. We bob on the sea, on the sea, on the beautiful sea, you and me, *you and me, oh how happy we'd be.*

She comes fiercely, head arched back, eyes closed. Her fingernails scratch a trail down to my ass, sharp, razor-thin strokes of passion. Longing. Desire. Home. *You and me, you and me, oh how happy we'd be.* Sirens wail in the distance. We lie still. I hold her. The sirens stop outside the window. A flashing red light circles around the living room walls. We sweat. And we breathe.

Ronny Cammerari says, "Love isn't perfeck. Love ruins

everything. Love breaks your heart." And I understand how true those words are. I love Sapphire. And everything is ruined. Our home, my trust, our love. I stroke her sweaty forehead, my other arm wound intimately around her. I have no idea what I want to do. I want our old life, but the past is past. And everything is different now. I want to kick her out, make her suffer the way I did. I want to kiss her, make love with her, lose myself in her sweet salty kisses, her familiar embrace.

A key turns in the lock. Betty walks in. Practically drops her iced mochaccino when she spots me and Sapphire naked on the couch. I smile meekly, embarrassed. She flashes a look that says she can't wait to hear about this, smiles, and heads for her bedroom. I squeeze Sapphire tighter. We watch the end of the movie in silence. And I decide not to decide anything, tonight.

About the Authors

Caril Behr was born in Cape Town, South Africa. Twenty-three years later she packed her bags and set sail for England. She now lives and works in North London, teaching art to adult students with special needs. Her short stories have appeared in *New London Writer* and *Queer Words*.

Robin Bernstein is an editor of *Bridges*, a biannual journal of Jewish feminist culture and politics. She is also the author of *Terrible, Terrible!*, a Jewish feminist children's book (Kar-Ben Publishing, 1998). Her first book, *Generation Q*, was a finalist for a Lambda Literary Award. Her work appears in Jewelle Gomez's and Tristan Taormino's *Best Lesbian Erotica 1997*, Susan Fox Rogers's *Women on the Verge: Lesbian Tales of Power and Play*, and many other anthologies. She lives with her partner in Washington, D.C.

Elana Dykewomon's novel *Riverfinger Women*, which features the first Jewish lesbian characters (after G. Stein), became one of the early classics of the women's movement's second wave. She went on to publish four other books, most recently *Nothing Will Be As Sweet As the Taste-Selected Poems* (Onlywomen Press, London), and the Jewish lesbian historical novel *Beyond the Pale* (Press Gang), nominated for the American Library Association G/L/B/T book award for 1997 and winner of a Lambda Literary Award. She brought the international feminist journal of arts and politics *Sinister Wisdom* to the San Francisco Bay Area, serving as an editor for nine years. She currently lives in Oakland with her lover, Susan, and shares the unexpected pleasures of a poodle, Gracie, with four friends.

Gabrielle Glancy's work has been published in *The New Yorker, The Paris Review, The American Poetry Review, Sister & Brother, Queer View Mirror 1 & 2, Hot & Bothered: Short Short Fiction on Lesbian Desire,* and many other anthologies. Her story "The Missing Letter" is part of a novel she is working on, which chronicles the sometimes comic, sometimes kinky exploits of a girl Casanova in search of her Russian lover who has mysteriously disappeared. She lives and writes in Tel Aviv, Israel.

Judith Katz is the author of two novels, *Running Fiercely Toward a High Thin Sound,* which won a Lambda Literary Award for best lesbian fiction, and *The Escape Artist.* Her work has appeared in numerous anthologies, including *Hot & Bothered* and *To Be Continued.* She teaches in the University of Minnesota Women's Studies Department and Hamline University's graduate MFA/MALS program. She is currently working on a third novel.

Jenifer Levin is the author of four novels, including *The Sea of Light*, which was a Lambda Literary Award finalist. Her first book, *Water Dancer*, published when she was twenty-six, was nominated for the PEN/Hemingway Award and helped establish her among the few contemporary uncloseted lesbian novelists to be published in and receive serious critical attention from the literary mainstream.

Joanna Lundy/Solomon is a Jewish lesbian and single parent of an eleven- year-old daughter. She lives in Vancouver, Canada, and works with street-involved youth. In her spare time, when she has any, she is a human rights activist and a writer. She has completed two creative documentaries and is currently working on her first novel. *Silence on Fire* is dedicated to those brave queer girls who love who they desire. Special thanks to Julie for being her writing buddy.

Margarita Miniovich is a Russian-born Jewish lesbian writer with many lives. At present, she is the managing editor of a Vancouver-based literary magazine, *The Capilano Review*. Her work has been published in *Fireweed*, a feminist literary journal, and she has given numerous readings in both Toronto and Vancouver. She wants to write, travel, have sex at least once a week, get two more cats and one more dog, and live in a wooden house facing a blue lake.

Lesléa Newman has published twenty-seven books, many of which have Jewish content, including the novel *In Every Laugh a Tear*, the short story collection *A Letter to Harvey Milk*, and the children's book *Matzo Ball Moon*. She is also the editor of *My Lover Is a Woman: Contemporary Lesbian Love Poems*, *Pillow Talk: Lesbian Stories Between* *the Covers,* and *The Femme Mystique.* Her newest title is a book of humor entitled *The Little Butch Book.*

Joan Nestle is the author of A Fragile Union: New and Selected Writings and A Restricted Country, She is the editor of *The Persistent Desire: A Femme-Butch Reader,* and co-editor of the award-winning *Women on Women* series and of the Lambda Award-Winning *Sister & Brother: Lesbians and Gay Men Talk About Their Lives Together.* She is the founder of the Lesbian Herstory Archives in New York.

Karen Taylor is a Jewish community worker in New York City, where she moved in 1996 after living in Seattle for ten years (and serving as Washington State Ms. Leather for 1994 and 1995). Her stories have also been published in *No Other Tribute* and *Leatherwomen III,* both edited by Laura Antoniou, and in *First Person Sexual,* an anthology of masturbation stories edited by Joani Blank. She is currently working collaboratively with Laura Antoniou on *Tales of the Marketplace,* a collection of short stories based on Antoniou's Marketplace series. Karen would like to thank Seattle's "No Safewords" Writers Group for their helpful criticism in the creation of this story.

Clara Thaler wrote her first poem at age six and her first piece of erotica at age fifteen. She recently received her undergraduate degree in sociology and is moving to Northampton.

About the Editor

Karen X. Tulchinsky is a nice Jewish lesbian and the award-winning author of *Love Ruins Everything*, a novel, and *In Her Nature*, a collection of short stories. She is the editor of *Hot & Bothered: Short Short Fiction on Lesbian Desire* and the co-editor of *Tangled Sheets: Stories & Poems of Lesbian Lust*, *Queer View Mirror 1 & 2: Lesbian & Gay Short Short Fiction*, and *To Be Continued*. Her work has appeared in numerous anthologies, including the Lambda Literary Award-winning *Sister & Brother: Lesbians and Gay Men Talk About Their Lives Together*, *Once Upon a Time*, and *Lesbians Raising Sons*. She has written for several magazines, including *Curve*, *Girlfriends*, and the *Lambda Book Report*. She lives and writes in Vancouver, Canada.

MORE BOOKS FROM CLEIS PRESS...

DEBUT LITERATURE
The Little School: Tales of
Disappearance and Survival ,
second edition, by Alicia Partnoy.
ISBN: 1-57344-029-9 14.95 paper.

Marianne Faithfull's Cigarette:
Poems by Gerry Gomez Pearlberg.
ISBN: 1-57344-034-5 12.95 paper

Memory Mambo by Achy Obejas.
Lambda Literary Award Winner.
ISBN: 1-57344-017-5 12.95 paper.

Queer Dog: Homo Pup Poetry,
edited by Gerry Gomez Pearlberg.
ISBN: 1-57344-071-X. 12.95. paper.

We Came All The Way from Cuba
So You Could Dress Like This?:
Stories by Achy Obejas.
Lambda Literary Award Nominee.
ISBN: 0-939416-93-X 10.95 paper.

Seeing Dell by Carol Guess
ISBN: 1-57344-023-X 12.95 paper.

MYSTERIES
Dirty Weekend: A Novel of Revenge
by Helen Zahavi.
ISBN: 0-939416-85-9 10.95 paper.

The Woman Who Knew Too Much:
A Cordelia Morgan Mystery
by B. Reese Johnson.
ISBN: 1-57344-045-0. 12.95 paper.

VAMPIRES & HORROR
Brothers of the Night: Gay
Vampire Stories
edited by Michael Rowe and
Thomas S. Roche.
ISBN: 1-57344-025-6 14.95 paper.

Dark Angels: Lesbian Vampire
Stories,
edited by Pam Keesey.
Lambda Literary Award Nominee.
ISBN 1-7344-014-0 10.95 paper.

Daughters of Darkness: Lesbian
Vampire Stories, second edition,
edited by Pam Keesey.
ISBN: 1-57344-076-0   14.95 paper.

Vamps: An Illustrtated History of
the Femme Fatale
by Pam Keesey.
ISBN: 1-57344-026-4 21.95.

Sons of Darkness: Tales of Men,
Blood and Immortality,
edited by Michael Rowe and
Thomas S. Roche. Lambda
Literary Award Nominee.
ISBN: 1-57344-059-0 12.95 paper.

Women Who Run with the Werewolves: Tales of Blood, Lust and Metamorphosis,
edited by Pam Keesey. Lambda Literary Award Nominee.
ISBN: 1-57344-057-4 12.95 paper.

SEXUAL POLITICS
Forbidden Passages: Writings Banned in Canada,
introductions by Pat Califia and Janine Fuller. Lambda Literary Award Winner.
ISBN: 1-57344-019-1 14.95 paper.

Public Sex: The Culture of Radical Sex
by Pat Califia.
ISBN: 0-939416-89-1 12.95 paper.

Real Live Nude Girl: Chronicles of Sex-Positive Culture
by Carol Queen.
ISBN: 1-57344-073-6. 14.95 paper.

Sex Work: Writings by Women in the Sex Industry, second edition,
edited by Frédérique Delacoste and Priscilla Alexander.
ISBN: 1-57344-042-6. 19.95 paper.

Susie Bright's Sexual Reality: A Virtual Sex World Reader
by Susie Bright.
ISBN: 0-939416-59-X 9.95 paper.

Susie Bright's Sexwise
by Susie Bright.
ISBN: 1-57344-002-7 10.95 paper.

Susie Sexpert's Lesbian Sex World,
second edition, by Susie Bright.
ISBN: 1-57344-077-9. 14.95 paper.

GENDER TRANSGRESSION
Body Alchemy: Transsexual Portraits
by Loren Cameron.
Lambda Literary Award Winner.
ISBN: 1-57344-062-0 24.95 paper.

Dagger: On Butch Women,
edited by Roxxie, Lily Burana, Linnea Due.
ISBN: 0-939416-82-4 14.95 paper.

I Am My Own Woman: The Outlaw Life of Charlotte von Mahlsdorf,
translated by Jean Hollander.
ISBN: 1-57344-010-8 12.95 paper.

PoMoSexuals: Challenging Assumptions about Gender and Sexuality
edited by Carol Queen and Lawrence Schimel. Preface by Kate Bornstein.
ISBN: 1-57344-074-4 14.95 paper.

Sex Changes: The Politics of Transgenderism
by Pat Califia
ISBN: 1-57344-072-8 16.95 paper.

*Switch Hitters: Lesbians Write
Gay Male Erotica and Gay Men
Write Lesbian Erotica,*
edited by Carol Queen and
Lawrence Schimel.
ISBN: 1-57344-021-3 12.95 paper.

*Lesbian and Gay Studies
Case of The Good For Nothing
Girlfriend: A Nancy Clue
Mystery,* 2nd edition,
by Mabel Maney.
ISBN: 0-939416-91-3. 14.95

*The Case of the Not-So-Nice
Nurse by Mabel Maney.*
Lambda Literary Award Nominee.
ISBN: 0-939416-76-X 9.95 paper.

*Chasing the American Dyke
Dream: Homestretch*
edited by Susan Fox Rogers.
ISBN: 1-57344-036-1 14.95 paper.

*A Fragile Union:
New & Selected Writings*
by Joan Nestle.
1-57344-040-X 14.95

*Nancy Clue and the Hardly Boys
in A Ghost in the Closet*
by Mabel Maney. Lambda Literary
Award Nominee.
ISBN: 1-57344-012-4 10.95 paper.

*Different Daughters:
A Book by Mothers of Lesbians,*
second edition,
edited by Louise Rafkin.
ISBN: 1-57344-050-7 12.95 paper.

A Lesbian Love Advisor
by Celeste West.
ISBN: 0-939416-26-3 9.95 paper.

On the Rails: A Memoir,
second edition,
by Linda Niemann. Introduction
by Leslie Marmon Silko.
ISBN: 1-57344-064-7. 14.95 paper.

SEX GUIDES
*Good Sex: Real Stories from Real
People,* second edition,
by Julia Hutton.
ISBN: 1-57344-000-0 14.95 paper.

*The New Good Vibrations Guide
to Sex: Tips and techniques from
America's favorite sex-toy store,*
second edition, by Cathy Winks
and Anne Semans.
ISBN: 1-57344-069-8 21.95 paper.

*The Ultimate Guide to Anal Sex
for Women* by Tristan Taormino.
ISBN: 1-57344-028-0 14.95 paper.

WORLD LITERATURE

A Forbidden Passion
by Cristina Peri Rossi.
ISBN: 0-939416-68-9 9.95 paper.

Half a Revolution: Contemporary Fiction by Russian Women,
edited by Masha Gessen.
ISBN 1-57344-006-X 12.95 paper.

COMIX

Dyke Strippers: Lesbian Cartoonists A to Z,
edited by Roz Warren.
ISBN: 1-57344-008-6 16.95 paper.

TRAVEL & COOKING

Betty and Pansy's Severe Queer Review of New York
by Betty Pearl and Pansy.
ISBN: 1-57344-070-1 10.95 paper.

Betty and Pansy's Severe Queer Review of San Francisco
by Betty Pearl and Pansy.
ISBN: 1-57344-056-6 10.95 paper.

Food for Life & Other Dish,
edited by Lawrence Schimel.
ISBN: 1-57344-061-2 14.95 paper.

WRITER'S REFERENCE

Putting Out: The Essential Publishing Resource Guide For Gay and Lesbian Writers, fourth edition, by Edisol W. Dotson.
ISBN: 1-57344-033-7 14.95 paper.

Since 1980, Cleis Press has published provocative, smart books - for girl-friends of all genders. Cleis Press books are easy to find at your favorite bookstore - or direct from us! We welcome your order and will ship your books as quickly as possible. Individual orders must be prepaid (U.S. dollars only). Please add 15% shipping. CA residents add 8.5% sales tax. MasterCard and Visa orders: include account number, exp. date, and signature.

How to Order
- Phone: 1-800-780-2279 or (415) 575-4700
  Monday - Friday, 9 am - 5 pm Pacific Standard Time
- Fax: (415) 575-4705
- Mail: Cleis Press P.O. Box 14684, San Francisco, California 94114
- E-mail: Cleis@aol.com